Of Masques and Murder

Of Masques and Murder

Maureen Klovers

For my sister, Christelle, my best critic and editor—and a
talented writer herself

ACKNOWLEDGMENTS

This book is dedicated to my sister, Christelle, who is the best sister and editor that one could ask for. She's got a lawyer's eye for detail, can spot an inconsistency a mile away, and always makes sure I'm true to the characters and the world I've created. She's also a terrific writer. I hope to see her historical fiction, short stories, and plays in print soon!

I also owe a debt of gratitude to my husband, Kevin Gormley; my mother, Mary Klovers; and my fellow author, Eileen Haavik McIntire, creator of *The 90s Club* cozy mystery series. They patiently helped me edit my manuscript and offered invaluable suggestions. Along with our daughter Kathleen, Kevin also served as a patient sous-chef, taste tester, and food photographer while I perfected the recipes for this book. He particularly liked the *torta pasqualina*!

I want to thank my dad, Kris Klovers, who gave me the great suggestion for a glossary; my friend Michael Glenn, who generously shared his wine expertise; my friend Justin Smith, who taught me about hunting blinds; reader Dianne Nickel Casey for suggesting one of the character's names (Orlando); and pharmacist Luci Zahray (aka "The Poison Lady") who has taught me and many other mystery writers how to (fictitiously!) poison our victims. At a mystery writers' conference in Dallas, Lucy patiently answered my questions about which plants could kill, what they could be confused with, where they'd grow, and how much I would need for a fatal dose.

Ken Leeder in the U.K. created my beautiful cover design.

That said, all mistakes in the book are my own.

Chapter One

Most Americans knew it as the season of Mardi
Gras, one last hurrah of devil-may-care exuberance
before the deprivations of Lent set in. But in the tight-
knit Italian-American community of Acorn Hollow, it
was Carnevale, and for once, Rita Calabrese longed to be
in New Orleans instead. It was not because New Orleans
celebrated Mardi Gras any better than Acorn Hollow
celebrated *Martedì Grasso*, which was exactly the same
thing except more authentic (the Romans invented the
holiday, not the French), with less debauchery (thank
heavens!), and with even more fattening and delicious
food. No, it was just because Rita wanted to be
somewhere warm and colorful, where the daffodils were
blooming, the farmers' markets would soon be springing
back to life, and the reporters were kept busy with one
juicy murder after another.

Acorn Hollow, in contrast, was bitterly cold and
blanketed in snow. Rita's rose bushes drooped under the
weight of the snow; the branches of her pear, apple, and
cherry trees were stark and barren against the gray skies;

and her garden plot lay fallow. It seemed as if spring would never come.

And there had not been a murder in the whole of Morris County in the past six months.

There had not been much of anything to report, in fact. Only two or three burglaries, all easily solved—especially that one in Mount Washington, where the burglar was still present, naked and eating a tuna fish sandwich when the police arrived. There had been only one measly local election, where the most shocking revelation was that one candidate had not actually baked the pie that she had entered into the local pie-making contest. (A non-issue, Rita thought, given that the pie in question had not even placed. Rita, of course, had taken home her eighteenth first-place title for her much-coveted sour cherry pie.) There had been no embezzlement allegations against local leaders, and no book-banning campaigns to rock the PTA. The *Morris County Gazette*'s biggest story all winter had been the record snowfall—and the fact that shoddy maintenance had rendered two of the county's snowplows inoperable at the worst possible time.

So it was no wonder that Rita, the *Morris County Gazette*'s star investigative reporter—and the county's most dogged sleuth, most prize-winning cook, and most renowned green thumb—was bored out of her mind. As an antidote, she threw herself into her family's preparations for Carnevale with even greater alacrity than usual, keeping her sous chefs—today, her husband and daughter—on task with near-military precision.

"Those lasagna noodles are too thick," she murmured, running her fingertips gently over the crimped edges as her daughter, Gina, rolled them off the pasta maker.

Gina rolled her dark eyes. She was a voluptuous brunette with a great job as vice president of the local bank, and she was a homeowner to boot. Rita couldn't understand why some quality young man—that is, a nice Italian boy who adored his mother and went to Mass every Sunday—didn't snap her up. Perhaps it was all that eye-rolling, although Rita presumed Gina saved most of that for her mother.

"So we'll boil them an extra minute, Ma. Jeez."

Rita reached over and turned the dial on the pasta maker down a few notches. "Your *nonna* used to always say that pasta should be—"

"*Così sottile per leggere un giornale giù.* Yeah, I know," Gina said. "Thin enough to read a newspaper through."

Rita laughed. "And all this time I thought you weren't listening, *figlia.*"

Rita gave her daughter an affectionate pat on the arm, then walked over to taste the meat sauce tended by her husband, Sal. Finding it too acidic, she threw in a pinch of sugar and then tore three glistening bright green leaves off the basil plant in the windowsill.

While pretending to look out the windows, as if admiring the foot of fresh white snow that blanketed the

Hudson Valley, Rita snuck a quick glance at the clock, then at her phone. She rummaged through the cabinets for a double boiler, filled the bottom with water, set it on the stove, and turned on the burner. With one eye on the phone, she plopped a bar of semisweet baking chocolate on the top of the double boiler, poured in some heavy cream, and began to stir.

At last, she heard the strains of "*Va, Pensiero,*" her very distinctive operatic ring tone.

"*Buon giorno!*" she trilled into the phone, nearly dropping it into the ganache in her excitement. "Oh, Marion, I didn't expect to hear from you today, what with Fred's brother visiting and all." Rita found it was really rather easy to tell a lie—just a fib, really—if it was in the service of the greater good. "I'm making the ganache for my flourless chocolate cake. Let me put you on speaker phone."

"Rita!" Marion bellowed in her distinctive, ear-splitting mezzo soprano. Marion was built like a battleship, and she had a voice to match.

"I called to share some rather sad news," Marion shouted, sounding anything but sad. "I just ran into Agnes Peruzzi at the grocery store. She was very upset. Apparently, Matt and Morgan broke up."

Little bubbles were beginning to form on the surface of the ganache mixture. Rita removed the ganache from the heat and, as she took her beautiful, velvety, deep dark chocolate flourless chocolate cake out of the refrigerator, she snuck a surreptitious glance at her daughter. Gina had dated Matt Peruzzi in high school, and Rita had always had a soft spot for him. She suspected that Gina still did, too. The main obstacle to their reunion had been that Morgan Abernathy had had her hooks in him for the past eight years. Morgan was a pretty girl, Rita supposed, if you were into skinny blondes with about as many curves as Rita's fettucine noodles. But pretty only gets you so far. Matt's mother had long since given up speculating when they would make it down the altar. And, now, he was finally free.

"Is Matt very upset?" Rita asked as she drizzled ganache onto the surface of the cake.

She noticed that Gina had stiffened for just a moment, her hand falling away from the crank on the pasta maker. But it was only for an instant. Then the mask slipped back and Gina began cranking out lasagna noodles once more.

"Oh, very," Marion said, "but he's determined to move on, to meet someone else. He signed up for dance lessons, apparently. Monday night tango lessons at Café Divorcée, Tuesday night salsa at the Mount Washington Community Center."

That last bit Mrs. Peruzzi had not exactly divulged at the grocery story; Rita had made use of her excellent sleuthing skills to get ahold of Matt's schedule.

"Just thought you should know, Rita," Marion bellowed, "in case you run into Agnes. Toodle-oo, then!"

Marion rang off. Rita poured the ganache over the cake, spread it carefully over the top and sides, and then sprinkled some pink Himalayan sea salt on top. She could feel Sal's glare on her and looked up in time to see his bushy salt-and-pepper beetled brows wagging a silent warning. In response, she shrugged in his direction as if to say: can I help it if a friend calls to tell me the latest gossip?

She turned her back to him. "There," she said triumphantly. "This will go splendidly with some homemade espresso gelato. You know, *cara*," Rita said to Gina as if she'd had a sudden inspiration, "maybe you should take some dance lessons. You always were so coordinated in gymnastics. And Matt was such a good friend of yours in high school."

"But I have yoga on Monday, and stitch-and—"

Rita raised a hand. She could not abide swearing.

Gina cleared her throat. "Knitting."

Yoga and knitting, Rita thought. That was the problem right there. How could her daughter ever meet a man when she spent all of her time in all-female environments?

"But you could take yoga on Wednesday instead," Rita said, "and you and your friends can knit any old time. I really think—"

"Ziti!" her husband suddenly hollered. "It's time for the ziti!"

"Ziti? Whatever are you talking about, Sal? One baked pasta should be plenty—"

"A word, *cara*." Sal took her roughly by the elbow and steered her towards the swinging door that led to the dining room.

On the other side of the door, he turned to her, red-faced and with that telltale vein bulging beneath his receding hairline.

"Ziti, Rita," he hissed. "It's our secret code word, remember? As in, not ziti, but *zitta*, as in '*stai zitta*.'"

His eyes, the color of maple syrup, glowered at her as he made the sign of a zipper closing over his lips. "*Stai zitta*" meant "be quiet" in Italian.

"I wouldn't say we agreed on it as a code word," Rita bristled. "You suggested it, but I never agreed."

He shook his head. "You told me, *cara*, that you were trying to repair your rather rocky relationship with our daughter. Remember that, *cara*? So no more conspiring with Marion. Gina can see right through it, and so can I." Sal grunted. "Besides, remember what happened the last time you tried to play cupid. You have to admit your taste in men is lousy."

Rita flushed to the silver roots of her bushy jet-black hair. "I married you, didn't I?" she said hotly. "Now, what happened with Gina's last beau was a fluke." She straightened her spine, gave him her most confident megawatt smile, and said breezily, "But you have a point, *caro*. I should go easy on her. She's hurting."

Rita sailed back through the swinging door, and Sal followed behind her. To her surprise, Gina's suspicious scowl had turned to a smile. Although Rita was not sure it was a smile she liked—it was more like the smug smile her two Bernese mountain dogs had when they'd successfully filched a *bistecca alla fiorentina*.

Gina looked up and said, "All this cooking for Carnevale has got me thinking about Lent. What's your *fioretto?*"

Fioretto literally meant "little flower" in Italian. It was a lovely little euphemism for whatever you had decided to sacrifice for Lent—the *fioretto* you were offering to God.

"Cigars," Sal said, and Rita felt a wave of relief. She hated brushing away the ashes scattered all over his basement man cave.

"What about you, Ma?"

"Oh, the usual. Chocolate."

Rita always gave up chocolate. It was truly penance for her, so she felt she was on solid ground spiritually. But it also helped her lose five pounds each spring.

"But that doesn't help the world really, does it?" Gina said, handing her mother a plate heaped with fresh lasagna noodles. "I mean, it's not as if the chocolate you give up feeds starving orphans in Africa. And if one really wanted to be cynical about it, it could all be construed as mere vanity. You want to lose a dress size."

"That is just a side benefit," Rita huffed. "But enlighten me, *figlia*. What should I give up?"

"Meddling."

The word hung heavily in the air. Rita was too shocked and affronted to immediately respond. Her husband, however, wagged a thick, stubby finger at his daughter. "Show some respect, *figlia*," he admonished her. "You're mother's not a meddler, anyway. She's, er"—

he glanced up at a spot on the ceiling, as if the perfect word hung there—"a problem-solver."

Sal's ears turned pink, suggesting he was not quite as convinced as he sounded, but Rita decided to give him a pass.

Rita beamed at her husband before turning to glare at her daughter. And then, in a fit of pique, before she'd had time to properly think it through, she suddenly declared, "Your father's right, Gina. I do not meddle. But if it will make you happy, I will give up *problem-solving* for Lent."

Chapter Two

With each passing hour, Rita's regrets multiplied. She could not tell what vexed her more—that she had forty days of sheer boredom ahead, or that her daughter was so thoughtlessly, so ungratefully contemptuous of Rita's problem-solving abilities.

"And just like that," she fumed to Marion, as she dropped little balls of dough into a vat of boiling oil, "Gina said 'meddling.' Like she didn't even have to think. Like it was premeditated."

They were in the cavernous industrial kitchen in the basement of St. Vincent's, making *bomboloni* for the hundreds of revelers who were outside watching the Carnevale procession and would soon come inside for thick Italian-style hot chocolate, mulled wine, and the exquisite Italian-style donuts called *bomboloni*.

"That Gina," Marion clucked, shaking her head. "Always thinking."

"Well, she should put that brilliant mind of hers to better use than thwarting her mother. Like getting a promotion—or a man."

Rita stuck a slotted spoon into the roiling liquid, scooped up several golden brown *bomboloni*, and lobbed them onto a tray of granulated sugar. They made a hissing, crackling sound as they hit the pan.

"I'm not even sure if it is a valid resolution," she muttered as she rolled each donut in sugar and arranged them on a tray. "I mean it wasn't so much a promise to God as appeasement of my daughter. A very ill-advised appeasement. And history tells us how that turned out."

Marion bit her lip as she handed Rita another perfectly round ball of dough. Rita could tell Marion was trying to work out the reference.

"World War Two?" Rita said. "Chamberlain? The Sudetenland?"

She was saved from having to further explain her analogy by the arrival of Father De La Pasqua. As the head of the procession, he was first in line for the *bomboloni*. Behind him were the men carrying a cart with a statue of St. Vincent covered in dollar bills, the shivering ballerinas dressed as swans for the Swan Lake float, and the members of the high school band. It had been a very eclectic parade—part religious, part community pride, part sheer silly fun.

"Padre!" Rita clapped her sugar-coated hands. "Just the man I wanted to see."

He raised his eyebrows and his expression of boyish excitement turned glumly pastoral. "Oh?"

"It's about my *fioretto*."

"Chocolate again?" He smiled, and two dimples appeared in his cheeks. "Well, you've got four more days, Rita, to squeeze in every chocolate dessert imaginable—gelato, truffles, your terrific chocolate flourless cake, maybe some tiramisu—"

"No, Padre, it's not that." Rita motioned him to come behind the counter, then huddled with him by the walk-in refrigerator. Lowering her voice, she went on. "I was going to give up chocolate as usual—which is very much a sacrifice for me, as you know."

"But you decided to give up something else this year, maybe something that could have a positive impact on others?"

Rita scowled. "I got tricked—coerced—into giving up...problem-solving. What some might mistakenly called 'meddling.'"

"I see." Father De La Pasqua quickly shoved some *bomboloni* into his mouth.

"Well? Can't I get some kind of annulment?"

He looked at her blankly.

"You know," she said, "like when a marriage doesn't work out, you can get an annulment. You can say, 'hey, I was duped about X, Y, and Z' and the church says, 'your marriage doesn't really count; you're free to walk away.'"

"Mmmm....well, I think the Pope might have a slightly different interpretation. But in any case, I'm afraid there is no process for annulling a Lenten resolution. That's really between you and God. Only you know if it's a truly worthwhile sacrifice that brings you closer to Him."

Rita smiled triumphantly. Well, she thought, I certainly didn't make that promise directly to Him—

"You know," Father De La Pasqua said, "the fact that you want so desperately to get out of this pledge makes it sound like this *would* be a real sacrifice for you." He clapped her on her slumping shoulders as her heart sank. "Look on the bright side, Rita. You can eat all the chocolate you want."

He hurried out to greet his parishioners, leaving her just standing there, speechless and dejected. Feeling like a condemned woman, Rita trudged back to her station by the hissing, sizzling vat of oil.

Only her place had already been taken by her twin sister, Rose, who was dropping balls of dough into the vat as fast as Marion could roll them, and then scooping them out and rolling them in sugar with a quick flick of the wrist.

"What's wrong with you?" Rose said. "You look shell-shocked."

After a moment's hesitation, Rita unburdened herself to her twin, all the while knowing she shouldn't. After all, Rose rarely took her side in family disputes. Rose was blunt in the extreme, and even more so with Rita, as if the fact that they had shared a womb rendered any filter completely unnecessary.

To her surprise, however, Rose just stared at her, dark eyes flashing, hands on her annoyingly svelte hips. "Well, you didn't agree, did you?"

"I was tricked."

"So you *did* agree?"

Rita nodded miserably. "And Father De La Pasqua wouldn't let me weasel out of it."

"*Sei pazza?*"

Rose rarely spoke their mother tongue, but "*sei pazza?*"—"are you crazy?"—was one of the few expressions she always said in Italian. Perhaps it was because of those hard, staccato "z's" which gave it that extra jolt of emphasis.

"And here I thought you'd be pleased," Rita said. "You of all people seem to think—wrongly, of course—that I meddle." On her sugary fingers, she ticked off all the epithets her sister had employed over the years. "You've called me Machiavelli, a Spanish inquisitor, a—"

"Yeah, yeah, yeah. Okay, so you intervene in your family members' lives at times and it drives them bonkers. But do you really have to quit *now*?"

"Now? What do you mean by 'now'?"

Rose took Rita by the elbow and started dragging her towards the rear of the kitchen. "We'll be back in a minute," she called out to Marion, one hand on the door to the walk-in refrigerator. Opening the door, she shoved Rita inside.

Rita leaned against a twenty-pound bag of tater tots, a staple of the school cafeteria. "*Sei pazza?* It's freezing in here."

"Yeah, well it's also private and sound-proof."

Rose folded her toned and now goosepimpled arms over her chest. Unlike Rita, who was dowdily but practically clad in corduroys, an old sweatshirt, and a "Kiss Me, I'm Italian" apron, Rose was wearing a fire engine-red sleeveless sheath, matching four-inch heels, and chunky gold jewelry. Between Rose's much svelter figure, fewer wrinkles (the benefit of having no husband or kids to worry about, plus lots of time for hot yoga), and short, expertly highlighted blond hair, many people didn't even realize Rita and Rose were identical twins.

"I need your help," Rose said.

"You want me to 'meddle'?"

"If you want to put it that way. You see"—Rose looked down, pretending to inspect one of her red talon-like fingernails—"I'm being blackmailed and you're good at tracking people down so I thought..."

"I could track them down so we could go tell Acorn Hollow's finest?"

"*Certo che non!* You think I want this to end up in court? No—so we can find out who it is, get dirt on him, and blackmail him to stop blackmailing me."

"What exactly is this person blackmailing you for?"

Rose wrinkled her nose. "I'll tell you on the drive."

"Drive?"

"To the Catskills. Think of it as just a scenic drive. It's beautiful this time of year with all that snow."

"Beautiful and dangerous," Rita said, thinking of the icy hairpin turns.

Just then the refrigerator door swung open. Rita's youngest son Vinnie stood there, his slight form shivering, his breath crystallizing. He had big puppy dog brown eyes, spiky black hair, and a wispy mustache he was inordinately proud of. He was her sweetest, most guileless child—and also the one she most blamed for her silver roots.

"Ma, Aunt Rose—what are you doing in here?"

"Just getting, uh,"—Rita looked around frantically, as tater tots were definitely not Carnevale food—"some more butter for the fryer."

"I thought you used oil."

Rita shrugged. "Adding in a little butter makes it even better. That was *nonna's* secret."

"Huh. Well, let me help you with that." He picked up a ten-pound tub of butter. "By the way, Ma, I heard you're giving up meddling or problem-solving or whatever you wanna call it for Lent. I wanted to say 'good for you, Ma.' That must be real hard for you."

Rita sighed. This was the ultimate backhanded compliment, although Vinnie didn't mean it that way. It was as good as an admission that he, too, thought she meddled.

"Four days," she muttered to Rose as they emerged back into the warmth of the kitchen and shut the refrigerator door behind them. "I've got four days and then...no interfering."

In other words, they had four days to get Rose out of the pickle she was in.

Chapter Three

Rita had only been back at her post by the boiling vat for twenty minutes when "*Va, Pensiero*" began to emanate from the depths of her apron pocket.

"Rita Calabrese, *Morris County Gazette*," she answered eagerly.

"I heard you took some kind of crazy no-meddling pledge," Sam, her editor barked. "The whole town is talking about it."

Rita could tell her editor was frowning deeply, which made Rita smile for the first time in two days. Finally, she had found the one sane person in Acorn Hollow who appreciated the sheer folly of such a pledge.

"It is crazy," Rita said with a contented sigh.

"Crazy and bad for business, Rita. I can't have my best reporter sidelined because of some kind of religious mumbo-jumbo."

Rita was not sure if it was because Sam was a Millennial, a lesbian, or one of the world's most cynical, skeptical people, but Sam was not a fan of organized religion, at least of the conventional sort. Instead, she seemed to gravitate towards a fascination with earth mother goddesses, the more obscure, the better.

"But I'm sure snooping for professional reasons doesn't count, right?" Sam continued. "I mean, separation of church and state, right? And what if you didn't snoop and, as a result, someone got away with murder? How would you like that on your conscience?"

Rita agreed that she would not. "Even Jesus performed miracles on the Sabbath," she acknowledged, "so I suppose some religious rules are meant to be broken—at least if there' s a very compelling reason."

"Work," Sam said severely, "is a very compelling reason. The survival of this paper—a beacon of light and truth arrayed against the forces of darkness and ignorance in Morris County—is a compelling reason."

That was surely hyperbole, but Rita was both pleased and alarmed to hear that the survival of the paper rested at least partly on her shoulders.

"Are there forces of darkness afoot in Morris County, though, at the moment?" Rita's tone was dubious, although hopeful. "It's been quite a slow news month."

"Not that I know of. But perhaps that's because they're so deep, so insidious, that only my toughest investigative reporter can ferret them out. Now," Sam said, "while you're figuring out exactly what dark forces are secretly at work, I need your help filling out next Sunday's edition, especially the food section. We're in that awkward time of year between 'light recipes to keep your New Year's diet' and 'let's make an Easter bunny cake.'"

Rita could hear the clicking of Sam's tongue ring against her teeth. The clicks got faster, signaling her impatience.

"Well?" Sam finally prodded. "You're the cook. What do you suggest?"

Rita frowned. They'd already run her recipes for chocolate-dipped peanut butter biscotti, the rather more traditional *cantucci*, and the ever-popular *pignoli* in a special on Italian-style cookies; a diverting treatise on foods used as aphrodisiacs around the world for Valentine's Day; and Rita's tips and tricks for perfect homemade pasta.

"It'll be maple sugaring season soon," Rita suggested. "Maybe I could pal around with a farmer tapping his trees."

"Sandy did that story last year. What else have you got?"

"Nothing grows this time of year, Sam," Rita said with a sigh. "Even you know that."

Everything Sam ate came out of a take-out box or a microwave.

"At least," Rita added, "nothing cultivated. I mean, there are a few things growing in the woods, I suppose."

"Brilliant!"

"You want me to do a story about a few clumps of shoots in the woods?"

"Foraging!" her editor shouted. There was a thump, and Rita could picture her editor's plump fist hitting her scratched-up dark wood desk. "It's apparently a thing now. People pay hundreds of dollars to eat seaweed and ants."

"I will most certainly *not* be eating ants."

"Fine. Just go find some foragers—preferably some weird aging hippies with shady pasts, maybe the kind who firebombed government labs or started cults—and go on an expedition with them. Take Rocco with you so he can get lots of close-ups of poisonous plants, the dangers that lurk in the forest. Amp up the drama."

Rita could hear the half-smile in Sam's voice, which by her editor's standards was a grin. "Who knows?" Sam said. "Maybe you'll trip over a dead body in the woods."

Chapter Four

Unfortunately for Sam, the organizer of Morris County's one and only foraging club was Viola Druther, the very picture of dull but cheerful respectability. She was annoyingly efficient and always had been, a born hall monitor and class secretary. Fifty years ago, she had caught Rita smoking in the girls' bathroom, startling Rita so much that she had accidentally set her beehive hairdo on fire. Rita had come away from the incident with singed hair, wounded pride, and a resolution to quit cold turkey—which she had kept so well that no one in her family even knew that she had smoked. But perhaps even more memorable was Viola's irritatingly indulgent smile and then the words that still smarted: "I'm supposed to report all incidents, of course, but I think you've learned your lesson."

In the intervening half century, Rita had steered clear of Viola and her relentless need to organize everyone and everything. They were civil when they met, Viola asking after Rita's family and Rita asking after Viola's cats and her job at the Rinaldi Winery.

But today Rita would have to be more than civil to Viola—she would have to ask her for a favor.

And she would do it, Rita decided, over a glass of Rinaldis' prize-winning red wine in their beautiful tasting room.

By her third pour, Rita was feeling quite mellow. The accompanying plate of brie and manchego cheese, fig jam, dried apricots, honey, and raisin crisps was delicious, intended for a crowd but oh-so-justifiable given that she had to drive home. And the view from the enclosed flagstone terrace was stupendous, with the Berkshires, hazy and purple, rising in the distance, and rolling forested hills in the foreground. The snow-covered branches were beautiful in their starkness, a geometric pattern against the cloudless blue sky. The newly-fallen snow sparkled in the sunshine, and there was a breathtaking clarity in the light of late winter, the tantalizing promise of spring just around the corner.

Out of the corner of her eye, Rita glimpsed Viola striding out of the storeroom, clipboard in hand. Clad in an expensive navy-blue blazer and crisp white shirt and swathed in pearls, Viola barked out orders (phased as helpful suggestions, although it fooled no one) with her trademark steely-lipped smile.

"Jack," Viola tut-tutted to a lanky, freckle-faced redhead, "you forgot to show the last customers the original bottle and cork when you poured the wine out of the decanter. We wouldn't want the customers to have a less than optimal tasting experience, would we?"

A few feet later, she snatched an antipasti platter right off a passing tray. "Presentation, presentation," she murmured with that same indulgent smile she'd used on Rita long ago. "This may taste good, but it doesn't look good. Send it back to the kitchen."

Finally, she got to Rita.

"Ah, Rita—it's good to see you. Sorry to keep you waiting. How's the family? I saw Vinnie the other day." She shook her head sadly and sighed. "Smoking. I guess he's a chip off the old block."

Rita couldn't believe Viola was still carping on the incident in the girls' bathroom. Drawing herself up to her full height, spine stiff as a rod, Rita made her reply through gritted teeth. "I haven't smoked in fifty years, Viola."

"Oh, well, that's splendid! Good for you. Such self-control."

It might have been Rita's imagination, but the last word seemed tinged with the teeniest bit of sarcasm as Viola took in Rita's "shareable"—and now nearly completely polished off—cheese plate.

"Really," Viola said, "it was one of those blessings in disguise. You lighting your hair on fire, that is. It made you quit cold turkey and, well, your hair bounced back as wild and unruly as ever."

Rita self-consciously patted a stray lock of hair back behind her ear.

"Now," Viola asked, "what can I do for you today?"

Finally, Rita thought with a sigh of relief, the polite chit-chat—which was anything but polite—was over.

"I wanted to write a story about foraging," Rita said, "and I hear you're the president of the local foraging club."

"So you want to interview me?"

"Shadow you, actually—tag along on a foraging expedition. Show our readers what's edible, what's poisonous, how to tell the difference. Maybe even share some tips about how to prepare foraged foods. Recipes, even."

"Well, you're in luck. I'm leading a group next week. It's an event open to the public, officially sponsored by Rinaldi's. We'll be bringing back some of the foods to the winery, having our participants compete to create the best dishes with those ingredients, and then serving those dishes with wine pairings. Orlando thought it could help us build some bridges to the community."

"Do you need to build bridges to the community?"

Viola shot Rita another one of her sad little smiles. "You would think we'd already built them, wouldn't you? With all the charity fundraisers we host, and the wonderful wine we produce, and our summer concert series. But some people are upset about our expansion plans. There aren't that many of them, but they're very vocal. They just aren't visionaries the way Orlando is."

Rita's ears perked up, sensing a story. "They're vocal? How so? I don't recall any letters to the editor about this."

"That would be the civilized way to go about it, wouldn't it? No, these are more the flame-throwing types—figuratively speaking, that is. They know that they can't get public opinion on their side, so they resort to more extreme measures. Harassment, really."

Rita was itching to take her notebook out of her purse, but she didn't want it to seem like an interview. "Oh?" she said casually. "Like what?"

Viola shrugged. "Nasty letters, graffiti, which we clean off immediately, of course—you name it. They fancy themselves some kind of noble eco-warriors. Claim they're concerned about increased traffic, light pollution, the increased use of pesticides." She sniffed and looked down her long, slightly horsey nose at Rita. "We use pesticides very sparingly, of course."

"Do you have photos of this graffiti? Can you show me some of the letters?"

"Oh, heavens, no! Orlando would not want that. He doesn't want direct confrontation; he wants a charm offensive. You catch more bees with honey, that sort of thing."

Rita's heart sank. There went Sam's coveted story on dark forces at work in Morris County. It wasn't murder, but at least it involved drama.

"So," Rita said, "you know who these, er, harassers are, then?"

"No, not at all. I mean, we know the type, of course—city folks who come up here and misguidedly want to preserve the valley in amber, who have lots of money but want to deny the residents of the valley—the original residents, that is—the ability to earn a good living, build a business, and create employment opportunities for locals." Viola patted Rita's hand. "But, then, I'm preaching to the choir."

Rita wasn't so sure about that, but since she wanted a story from Viola, she decided to keep mum.

"Anyway," Viola said, "those are just the types who will get excited about foraging. So Orlando—"

Viola stopped abruptly in mid-sentence. Rita followed her distracted gaze to the bar, where Jack, the hapless young redheaded employee who'd been on the receiving end of Viola's earlier tut-tutting, was talking with a thin, long-faced young man in shiny black shoes and black jeans that looked like they had actually been pressed.

Viola crooked her finger in their direction, and Jack came scurrying over, leaving the other young man at the bar.

"Yes, Ms. Druther?" He wrung his hands anxiously, seemingly eager to please.

"Tell Pierre-Claude," Viola said imperiously, "that we need three more wheels of brie, two of parmesan, two of gouda, and one of manchego. Let's not order any more sharp cheddar for now—it doesn't go with our new late winter menu."

Jack flushed so deeply that his freckles almost disappeared. Rubbing his ginger stubble, he said, "Greta—that is, Ms. Giroux—gave me the new cheese order yesterday."

"And was it exactly what I just said?"

Jack looked down at his scuffed shoes. "Well, not exactly..."

Viola patted Jack on the arm. "Trust me, Jack, I've been with Orlando thirty years. I know what he wants before he wants it. Greta...well, she's only known him—what?—a year?"

There was an uncomfortable silence. Rita found it interesting that Viola used the phrase "been with Orlando" rather than "worked for Orlando." The subtext was more than clear. Viola had outlasted the first Mrs. Rinaldi—a haughty, high-maintenance woman who hated everything about Orlando except his ability to pay generous court-ordered alimony—and she would outlast this parvenu as well.

"Now, run along," Viola said, dismissing him. "And tell Pierre-Claude exactly what I said."

Viola turned back to Rita. "That's Jack MacDougall. He's new," she said with a sigh. "He's only been here a few months. Eventually he'll learn how things are done around here. Will you be staying for dinner? Tonight, we have a lovely rack of lamb with red wine sauce and roasted root vegetables."

Rita wished she could. It would be lovely dining there beside the roaring fire as dusk turned to a clear starry night. But she had just fifty-five hours left to help her sister—and, tonight, they had a *rendezvous* in the mountains.

Chapter Five

Rita had not thought it possible to be more uncomfortable than she had been on the white-knuckle ride deep into the heart of the Catskills, her whole body continuously braced for impact. They had skidded on black ice twice, regaining control just in time to avert certain disaster. Then, they'd narrowly missed a collision with a giant buck who, either curious or suicidal, leapt out of the forest and bounded straight towards them, his eyes gleaming in their high beams. The deer hopped away at the last second as Rita desperately pumped the brakes.

But now her sixty-seven-year-old body was folded like an accordion in a draughty, bone-chillingly cold, rickety deer blind that creaked ominously beneath her each time the wind blew. Her twin's kneecap was jutting into her hip, and the small of her back was wedged against a wooden beam. She sunk down lower and pulled the flannel blanket further up her neck, then took a sip of lukewarm espresso from her thermos.

"I can't believe you roped me into this," she muttered. "And how could you be so stupid, so naïve? Skinny-dipping in a client's hot tub? Didn't you watch that *Dateline* special about how there are hidden cameras everywhere?"

"No," Rose said drily, "because I am never home at eight o'clock on a Friday night."

"Well, maybe if you were," Rita said pointedly, "you wouldn't be in this predicament."

Rita poured more espresso into her little plastic cup. She took a cookie tin out of her bag, snatched a homemade chocolate-dipped peanut butter biscotti, and dunked it in the espresso.

"So," Rita asked, "who were you with?"

"Paolo, of course."

"Who?"

"Paolo. You met him at my New Year's party. He told you your *arancini* tasted just like his *nonna's*."

Rita has a vague memory of chatting with a ridiculously good-looking archaeology professor from Naples who was teaching at NYU that year. He was tall and broad-shouldered, with perfectly bronzed skin and smoldering green eyes, and he was at least ten years Rose's junior. He had struck Rita as an outrageous flirt. He spoke with an incredibly sexy accent—exaggerated, Rita guessed—and expansive hand gestures that often ended with him gently brushing his fingers against his female conversation partner.

"Oh, *that* Paolo," Rita said. "Sal didn't like him. He said he was way too 'handsy.'"

"No man likes him," Rose said with a dreamy look on her face. "They simply can't compete."

"I didn't get the idea it was serious."

"Who said it was serious?"

"But you were in a hot tub with him in nothing but your—your—birthday suit!" Rita sputtered. "*Mamma* would be rolling over in her grave."

For once, Rose didn't even try to argue the point. Their mother had been a daily-Mass-attending, rosary-praying saint, chaste and modest as they come. She always maintained that their father was the only man she had ever kissed, and even then only after their engagement.

Scooting over to the slit in the deer blind, Rita peered outside and down at the "boulder"—really just a cleverly disguised hollow chunk of plastic—into which they had deposited fifty crisp twenty-dollar bills after, of course, writing down their serial numbers. Rita felt a grudging admiration for the blackmailer—he had chosen a drop date that coincided with the new moon. Beneath a clear, starry sky, the forest was shrouded in darkness.

What the blackmailer had not counted on, however, was that Rose would enlist the services of someone with access to night-vision goggles. Rita had borrowed them from an Iraq war vet with a weakness for her chocolate-dipped peanut butter biscotti. "Don't ask, don't tell" she'd said as she slid a huge tin of biscotti across the table. And he'd had the good sense not to.

Rita peered through the goggles and, seeing nothing except a squirrel scampering across the path, settled back onto the floor.

"So, start from the beginning," Rita said. "When did the blackmailer first contact you?"

"Three weeks ago. There was a large pink envelope in my mailbox that had my name on it, but nothing else—not my address, not a return address."

"Typewritten or written by hand?"

"Calligraphed. At first, I thought maybe it was a hand-delivered invitation to a wedding or a baby shower. It looked festive, you know? But I didn't recognize the handwriting, and I couldn't think of anyone I knew getting married or having a baby."

Rita nodded ruefully. She didn't either, much as she'd like her daughter Gina to get married, or her son Marco and his wife to give her a grandchild.

"So I took it inside," Rose said, "slit it open, and out fell the photos."

"And these photos appeared to be from a security camera?"

Rose shook her head. "No, I really don't think so. They weren't grainy at all."

"Could you tell where the photographer was standing when they were taken?"

"Probably near the fence. I went back the next day, looking for footprints in the flowerbeds, but it had snowed. All I found was a wadded-up receipt for the Sunshine Café."

31

Rita's ears perked up. Fran Zefferrelli, the owner of the Sunshine Café, was heavily indebted to Rita—literally and figuratively. Rita had helped Fran beat a murder rap and was also the guarantor of the restaurant's mortgage.

But before Rita could even ask, Rose reached into her pocket, extracted a wad of tissue-thin paper, and unfurled it while squinting at it with her pocket flashlight. "Cup of coffee, Cobb salad, iced tea, January twenty-first. Table seventeen; Roxanne was the server."

With a frown, Rita realized Roxanne was unlikely to remember who had ordered that a whole month before.

"And what about the note? What did it say?"

Rose took out a Ziploc bag and handed it, and the pocket flashlight, to Rita. With a gloved hand, Rita fished out the pink envelope first. Just as Rose had said, it was blank except for the words 'Rose Mancini' in a beautiful meticulous script.

Rita lifted it up and sniffed it. She detected nothing—no perfume, no aftershave.

She was just reaching for the note when a crackling sound caused Rita and Rose to spring to their feet, grab the night-vision goggles, and press their faces against the slit in the deer blind.

Rita held her breath as a dark, shadowy figure approached the plastic boulder, then looked around nervously, but unfortunately not up. Their vantage point was ideal, she supposed, to kill a deer—or a person. But the angle was too high to get a clear view of anything but the top of the individual's head, which was covered in a dark stocking cap.

Rita fiddled with her phone for a moment, cupping her hand over the pocket flashlight. She took off her glove for just a moment, and the icy wind shot through her. Then she stabbed 'play,' and a horrible screeching sound filled the air.

That did the trick. The man looked up, one hand poised above his forehead as if ready to strike an incoming flight of Hitchcock's birds.

In the split second between lowering his hand and looking down again, Rita glimpsed dark, slightly almond-shaped eyes, a long slightly crooked nose that flared out at the bottom, fleshy lips, and a neatly trimmed black beard. The man's face was ruggedly handsome, and his stocking cap was emblazoned with 'Patriots.'

And Rita had seen enough to know that, underneath the hat was a shaved head, as smooth and as hard as a billiard ball.

The twin sisters turned to each other and mouthed his name in unison. "Orlando Rinaldi."

Rita was shocked; she would never have taken Orlando for a blackmailer. She held her breath as he crouched down in the snow, turned the boulders over, and slid open the plastic panel.

But then he did something totally unexpected.

He reached into his pocket and pulled out a plastic bag. It had been wrapped around itself several times and was about the size of a brick. He placed it inside the panel, slid it shut, and returned the boulder to its spot on the ground.

Looking furtively around once more, he shoved his hands in his pockets and headed back down the path, his boots crunching in the snow.

He was a victim too, then.

Stunned, Rita leaned back against the wall and pulled the flannel blanket tightly around her. The wind rattled through the bare branches, and an owl hooted in the distance.

"What could he possibly be blackmailed for?"

Rose shrugged. "Same thing, maybe. Naughty photos of him and Greta. Or, worse, him and someone else. That might derail the wedding."

"That doesn't strike me as something Orlando would do. Marie was impossible, and he never cheated on her."

"Maybe the blackmailer's got ammo that Marie could use against him, then. Something to re-open the divorce settlement. Maybe he hid some assets from her."

Rita frowned. She'd always liked Orlando, but she supposed it was possible. Perhaps she was blinded by the fact he was the father of Gina's good friend Bianca. Rita had shared her espresso and biscotti with Orlando on many a raw, wet, blustery sideline. Marie usually spent the girls' soccer games in her limo, with the heat running full blast. While a firm believer in the sanctity of one's marriage vows, Rita hadn't felt that badly when Orlando and Marie announced they were getting divorced. She'd always thought Orlando could do better—and now, with Greta, she hoped he had.

Rita poured herself more espresso, brought it to her lips, and made a face. It was cold now. She was cold, too—frozen to the very marrow of her bones.

She slipped on a handwarmer, then pulled her gloves on top. Gingerly, she fished out the blackmailer's note and brought it close to her face. The light from the travel flashlight illuminated a jumble of odd fonts and sizes. "Mirror, mirror on the wall," it read. Each letter had been cut out of a magazine and painstakingly glued on notebook paper. "Who is the trampiest of them all? If you don't want these photos to see the light of day, you must pay. Deposit $1000 here by midnight next Monday."

Beneath was a beautifully drawn map of the forest, showing the plastic boulder beside the intersection of Trickling Springs Trail and the Old Chestnut Fire Road.

"So all we've got to go on," Rita muttered, "is the fact the person is familiar with 'Snow White and the Seven Dwarves,' and this spot in the woods. He or she is visually artistic, but a terrible poet. And he or she is a perfectionist. See?" Rita waved the paper in Rose's face, forgetting that, without the flashlight, it was illegible. "The bottom of each cut-out letter lines up perfectly with the lines on the paper."

"I wonder—" her sister began, but Rita cut her off with a swift silencing gesture as someone else approached.

This time, it was a woman. Limp, light-colored hair flowed out from beneath her stocking cap, and she wore a cinched-waist ski jacket, jeans, and dark boots. She too crouched down and slid a wadded-up plastic bag into the boulder, then straightened up and brushed the snow off her jeans. Look up, Rita silently willed her.

But the woman did not. She turned to walk back through the forest as Rita stabbed furiously at her phone. But nothing happened.

Rita felt around the floor until her fingers closed around a clump of acorns—presents, she surmised, from the squirrels she and Rose had displaced. With as much force as she could muster, Rita lobbed an acorn at the woman, hitting her between the shoulder blades.

The woman stiffened, then spun around, scanning the trees for a furry attacker. A beautiful face—a beautiful familiar face—filled Rita's scope.

The night-vision goggles made everything different shades of green. But Rita knew what that face looked like in full color—stunning, long-lashed turquoise eyes, high cheekbones, and bee-stung pale pink lips, against a backdrop of honey blond tresses.

It was a face that combined childlike innocence and wonder with womanly wiles.

A face (and a body) that could make men weak-kneed.

Greta Giroux.

Rita's jaw dropped. The fact that Orlando and Greta had arrived separately, thirty minutes apart, suggested that neither knew that their intended was being blackmailed.

Which suggested that each was harboring a terrible secret from the other.

Rita watched her slim figure retreat into the darkness, the footfalls fading in the distance.

"Well," Rose muttered, "at least I'm in good company. I wonder who'll show up next."

But the next several hours passed uneventfully. Serenaded by hooting owls, growling bobcats, and howling coyotes, the two sisters traded gossip, played *briscola* with a deck of Italian playing cards, and debated whether Gina was going to end up with Matt Peruzzi or not.

But just as Rita drowsily inserted her last handwarmer and the sun's tepid rays peeked over the horizon, there was a snapping sound below, as if someone had stepped on the branch Rita had placed beside the boulder.

Rita scrambled for her goggles and blinked as the figure, looming large in her scope, reached into the plastic boulder and pulled out several bricks of cash.

Elbowing Rose, she whispered, "Finally—our blackmailer."

The figure's wool double-breasted coat was beautiful, but not particularly distinctive. But the jaunty beret—red, she guessed—was perched on a severe dark bun that looked strangely familiar.

She lobbed an acorn, and it whizzed through the crisp, dry air and thwacked the woman in the head.

Rita felt a stab of guilt, then reminded herself that it was an accident and, besides, she was doing this all for the greater good.

The face looked up and squinted.

Rita gasped.

Viola Druther was looking right at them.

Chapter Six

A half an hour later, Rita and Rose were headed down the mountain, the heat in Rita's car turned up to full blast. But Rita's hands would not stop shaking as she clutched the steering wheel. She had never been so cold in her life, or so afraid of getting in a car accident, or even so surprised.

"Viola!" she exclaimed for the hundredth time. "A blackmailer!"

"I should have known it was a woman," Rose muttered. "No man would be able to calligraph an envelope so beautifully."

"But why blackmail *you*? Viola barely knows you."

"Well, we were classmates." Rose's dark eyes narrowed and she rubbed her temples, as if searching her memory. "I think maybe we were in gym together, maybe freshman English, too. But I never got the impression that she hated me in particular." She snorted. "But she kind of seemed to hate everyone. She acted like she was the warden and we were the prisoners. I've never seen a hall monitor so drunk on power."

"Could it be as simple as that? Viola just misses her hall monitor days and wants that power back? She wants to lord it over people?"

"Maybe."

"That seems so petty for someone our age."

"Yes—but not out of character for Viola."

"But still—why you? I doubt she just happened upon you and Paolo. She went to a lot of work to get those pictures."

"Maybe she's jealous. We're the same age, and she's a dried-up spinster and I'm"—Rose smacked her lips—"a sex goddess with a hot, younger Italian boyfriend."

Rita sighed and, for just a nanosecond, sympathized with Viola. Sometimes her sister's opinion of herself was just a mite too high. Rose was very attractive for her age, but a sex goddess? That was a stretch. Still, she might be on to something...if it were just her and Greta. Because Greta was most definitely a sex goddess and someone Viola might resent.

"But then," Rita said, "how do you explain her blackmailing Orlando? She adores Orlando, and you can't tell me she hates him for being a sex goddess."

"Maybe she just hates people who are in love."

"You're in love with Paolo?"

"Well, he's in love with me, at least."

Rita emitted a sound halfway between a laugh and a grunt. "*Poverino*," she muttered, shaking her head. "*Poverino Paolo*." He was going to leave America with a broken heart.

They had finally arrived at the base of the mountain, and Rita sighed with relief. The road stretched out before them, gently undulating, the silver shimmer of the Hudson peeking over the horizon, acting as a beacon towards home.

Home. Rita wanted nothing more than to crawl into her nice warm bed and dream of something—anything—more pleasant that Viola Druther.

"I hate to say it," she said as she hit the accelerator, "but Viola might be the worst possible blackmailer for your plan. What kind of dirt can we dig up on Miss Perfect?"

An hour later, the weak winter sun already high in the sky, Rita sunk down further under the covers and relished the feeling of soft fur on her frozen toes. Sal didn't allow the dogs in their bed, but Rita reasoned that this was a medical emergency.

"After all," she muttered darkly, "my toes could turn black and fall off. Would Sal be happy about his fur-free bed then? It'd be awfully hard for me to rush around making his gnocchi and cannoli and *struffoli* in a wheelchair."

Cesare nestled even closer, as if agreeing with her wholeheartedly.

Rita felt her eyelids drooping, her head sinking deeper into the fluffy down pillows. "Do you think," she murmured drowsily to her canine companions, "Viola saw us?"

She felt a lump of fur shake at her feet. Judging by the little snores emanating from somewhere in the vicinity of her toes, Luciano and Cesare were probably both asleep and the shaking was not so much a "no" as a

physical manifestation of a very good dream chasing
bunnies.

But Rita chose to interpret it as an affirmation.
"No," she said, "I don't think so either. The slit was tiny,
and we'd already turned off the flashlight...."

And then there were three creatures snoring
beneath Rita and Sal's duvet.

****

The arrival of the garbage truck—announced with a
deep rumble and then a sharp beep-beep-beep—jolted all
three out of bed. Serenaded by frantic yelps of
anticipation, the pounding of eight paws on the carpeted
staircase, and then the thwack-thwack-thwack of the dog
door opening and shutting, Rita pried open an eyelid
and struggled to make sense of the wavy lines on the
clock.

How long had she slept?

She fumbled for her glasses, slid them on, and
blinked a few times.

It was nearly two o'clock.

Which meant she had only thirty-four hours to get
Rose out of her predicament before Lent began.

Rita threw on an outfit as black as her mood,
topped it with a wool sweater (she was *still* cold), and
shuffled down the stairs and into the kitchen.

Luciano and Cesare leapt back through the
swinging dog door, tails wagging in ecstasy, crumbs on
their lips, and bounded across the hardwood floor,
skidding to a stop at her feet.

"You know," Rita said, "in some ways, you are far
superior to my human children. You're always happy,

always affectionate—and you would never make me take some silly pledge not to meddle."

Both dogs raised their ears and cocked their heads, as if earnestly trying to understand.

"Which," Rita added as she stabbed the button on her espresso machine, "I don't."

In record time, Rita knocked back her piping-hot espresso, wolfed down two chocolate-drenched peanut butter biscotti, walked Luciano and Cesare around the block, leapt behind the wheel of her green Buick, and careened down the windy country lanes to the winery.

This is the moment of truth, Rita thought as she got out of the car and trudged across the gravel parking lot. I'll know the moment I see Viola if she saw me last night or not.

Of course, Rita had absolutely no idea what she was going to do or say if Viola had seen her. Nor did she have a ready excuse of why she was there. To try the rack of lamb with red wine sauce and roasted root vegetables? But that wouldn't give her an excuse to size up Viola.

She had reached the steps. She took them slowly, the wheels turning in her mind, her breath coming out in little white puffs.

Rita heard footsteps behind her and then felt something brush against her shoulder.

"Oh, sorry."

The voice was of a young man. Out of the corner of her eye, she recognized the redheaded, freckle-faced boy that she had met during her last visit to the winery. He had a half dozen elaborate costumes hoisted up on his shoulder.

"They're for St. Vincent's masked Carnevale ball," Jack said apologetically. "Greta and Orlando asked me to pick these up from the cleaners."

"Six costumes for two people?"

"I know, right? But this is just a tiny bit of Orlando's collection. He's got dozens of Carnevale costumes. Maybe even a hundred."

"A hundred?" Rita exclaimed with a gleam in her eye. "I had heard," she lied, "about his collection, of course, but I didn't know it was that large. That's why I'm here, actually. To interview him about Carnevale costumes for tomorrow's special edition of the *Morris County Gazette.*"

She bit her lip. "I should have called ahead, but...."

She trailed off, searching for a reason. But Rita needn't have worried.

"No problem," he said, taking her by the arm. "I'm sure Orlando would love to talk to you." He winked. "Provided you mention our special Carnevale brunch tomorrow."

Chapter Seven

Half an hour later, Rita was relaxing by a roaring fire in Orlando's cozy and very masculine office—all dark wood and comfy furniture, like something out of Sherlock Holmes—with a cheese plate on her lap and a mug of mulled wine in her hand. She was so entranced by the parade of exquisite Carnevale costumes that she periodically forgot to take notes.

"Carnevale," Orlando was explaining, "is a corruption of the words '*carne*' and '*levare*.'"

He didn't translate the words for her, since he knew he didn't need to. '*Carne*' meant meat, and '*levare*' meant to raise or take away. In other words, it was the beginning of the meatless season of Lent.

Orlando rolled up his sleeves and wiped a bead of sweat off his shaved head. It was hot by the fire, gloriously hot after the bracing cold of the night before. Rita wondered if that's why he had lit the fire—to rid himself of the memory of last night, when the threat of blackmail had lured him to a remote snow-covered wood.

He didn't look tormented, though, nor did he look like a man harboring secrets.

Orlando said, "What we think of as Carnevale, though—the bacchanalia that precedes Lent—started in Venice in 1162, when the citizens went wild celebrating the victory of the Republic against the Patriarch of Aquileia. Everyone just began dancing spontaneously in Piazza San Marco."

Rita smiled, thinking of her one and only trip to Italy, when she had sloshed through the piazza in her galoshes—Venice was in the midst of one of its periodic *acque alte*—and first gazed upon the lions standing guard over San Marco. It had been pure magic, and not even the ensuing downpour had dampened Rita's spirits. She and Sal had danced too, splashing like two kids in a paddling pool, slightly tipsy from one too many glasses of Prosecco.

"From then on, it became an annual celebration," Orlando said as Rita scribbled down notes, determined not to be distracted by a walk down memory lane.

"And why did the costumes become so elaborate?"

"Ah, the costumes. During Carnevale, the sumptuary laws were suspended. See, normally, the church and the civil authorities—which were joined at the hip, of course—regulated what everyday people could wear. They didn't want common folk putting on airs. But during Carnevale those laws were suspended. So people could wear whatever they liked—and they did. And pretty soon"—he grinned—"all of the normal rules of behavior went out the window, too. For two weeks each year, people engaged in all kinds of wanton behavior, conveniently hidden behind a mask—or a whole

46

costume. Now, many of the costumes are really just lovely ball gowns that would have been in vogue among the upper class of Venice during the Republic's Golden Age." He ran a hand lovingly over the plush burgundy, emerald green, and royal blue velvet gowns that were draped over the back of the sofa. "Worn with a mask, of course, and perhaps an elaborate headdress."

"Like that?" Rita pointed at a frighteningly pale, oversized mask with a grotesquely protruding jawline.

Orlando laughed. "Well, most women opt for a small velvet mask, something more sexy than scary. That's a *bauta* mask, normally worn with a tricornered hat and a black cape. The mask sticks out like that to distort the wearer's voice. That's when you really want to get up to some mischief without anyone knowing who you are."

Rita laughed uneasily. She wondered just what mischief Orlando had been up to. Viola, she thought with a shudder, was certainly in a position to know. They'd worked together for decades.

"Are you going to wear that?" Rita asked, trying to sound as if she were joking. "So you can get up to some mischief?"

"Oh, no. I'm a straight arrow, as you know. All I have time for is work—and my family."

He said this without a trace of irony or hesitation.

"Given that you're about to get married," Rita said, "you might want to reverse that."

Orlando smiled. "I do have a lovely fiancée, don't I? After Marie, well..." He trailed off, then shook his head ruefully. "'If you don't have anything nice to say, don't say anything at all.' That's what my mamma always used to say."

"Wise words from a wise woman." Rita smiled. She always liked a man who listened to his mother. "I hope you and Greta will be very happy."

She meant that sincerely but, knowing that both Orlando and Greta were being blackmailed, she rather doubted it. What was Greta hiding behind that lovely visage? And what did anyone really know about her? She'd only been in Acorn Hollow a little over a year. That was a mere blink of the eye in the upper Hudson Valley, where most families went back at least a hundred years and many could trace their lineage to the old families of New Amsterdam.

Rita pointed at an even more frightening outfit consisting of a long black robe, black gloves, and a white mask with a long, grotesque curved beak and two milky, semi-translucent jewels set in the eye sockets. Anyone wearing that would not have a single pore of skin exposed—not even an eyeball. There was something particularly sinister about the costume. It seemed like the garb of a judgment figure, someone cold and detached from humanity.

"*Medico della peste*," Orlando said, tracing the long beak with a thick, hairy finger, as Rita shuddered once more. "The plague doctor—not just a costume, but very much a real person in the Middle Ages and Renaissance. Europeans believed in the miasmic theory—that 'bad airs' brought the plague. So doctors attending plague victims dressed like this, so that they wouldn't breathe in the bad airs. The beak is hollow, and there's room inside for lavender to mask bad odors—which they thought of as synonymous with bad air."

He chuckled. "They were wrong, but in a sense they were right. The plague is transmitted by rats, not bad air, but the costume actually did partly protect doctors from getting sick. It covered everything, absolutely everything."

With Orlando's permission, Rita took out her camera and snapped a few photos of the costumes. Her photos wouldn't turn out nearly as well as if they'd been taken by Rocco, the *Morris County Gazette*'s official photographer, but they'd do.

She was just snapping a photo of the *medico della peste* costume when the door to Orlando's office opened and Viola strode in, head buried in a clipboard. Rita froze like a deer in headlights.

"We've got eighteen tables reserved for lunch tomorrow," Viola said. "The champagne is being chilled in the cellar, the chocolate pots de crème have been made, and—" Suddenly, she looked up. "Oh, I thought you were alone."

Swallowing hard, Rita forced herself to look intently at Viola. Had Viola gotten a glimpse of her and Rose last night? Did Viola know that Rita knew she was blackmailing her employer and his fiancée?

But Viola just said, "Hello there, Rita. Excuse the interruption."

Viola's expression was her normal prim look mingled with a touch of smug superiority. She did not look the slightest bit worried or alarmed or embarrassed.

Either she was a great actress or she hadn't seen them; Rita guessed the latter.

"Hello there, Viola." Rita peered over her glasses at Viola. "You're looking a little tired. Have a long night last night?"

"Just curled up with my cat and a good book," Viola said with a tight-lipped smile.

"Really? What book? If it's good enough to keep you up at night, I should read it."

"Oh, just an Agatha Christie."

"Viola is quite the reader," Orlando said with an admiring smile.

Viola blushed, and Rita wondered if she was blushing because she was ashamed of blackmailing someone so fond of her, or blushing out of pleasure at his compliment.

"You two know each other so well," Rita observed. "How long have you worked together?"

"Twenty-one years," Viola blurted out at the same time as Orlando said "twenty."

Orlando laughed. "Must be twenty-one," he said. "Viola knows everything."

Yes, Rita thought, more than you know, but out loud, Rita just murmured, "Longer than most marriages."

"Longer than my marriage to Marie, certainly," Orlando said. "That lasted nineteen years. Oh, well"—Orlando attempted a laugh—"on to the next marriage. Hopefully I'll have better luck this time."

Viola flushed again. She spun on her heels to go but found her exit blocked by the future Mrs. Rinaldi.

"Speak of the devil," Viola muttered, just loud enough for Rita to hear.

Greta must have heard it too, but she pretended she didn't. "The flowers for tomorrow are here," she announced. Her honey-blond hair was as beautiful as ever, but there were dark circles beneath her eyes—courtesy, Rita surmised, of a sleepless night tramping through the woods. "But they're white oleander, and we ordered roses, so I'm going to—"

Viola held up a hand. Both women were now facing off against Orlando and seemed to have forgotten Rita was even there.

"Oh," Viola said, "I changed the order."

A frown line creased Greta's luminous, milky white forehead. "You—what?"

"Roses are just too prosaic. I thought white oleander would give the luncheon more of a sense of occasion."

"Orlando?" Greta said impatiently.

Orlando was drumming his fingers on the back on the couch. "Mmmm," he said absentmindedly. "Well, I guess oleander it is. Viola is so good at organizing these things."

Greta shot Viola a murderous look. She crossed in front of her, very close, and planted a loud kiss on Orlando, as if marking her man.

"See you in a few minutes," she said pointedly to Orlando and, ignoring Viola and Rita, left the room.

Well, there's a motive for blackmail, Rita thought. Greta is threatening Viola's position as queen of the castle.

Chapter Eight

Rita and her entourage—Sal, her children, and her eldest son Marco's wife, Susan—stood on the landing halfway down the stairs and looked down on the sea of Carnevale revelers. St. Vincent's cavernous basement was normally a sterile, harshly lit expanse of linoleum floor, crammed with battered lunch tables and smelling of tater tots and bleach. But tonight, it had been transformed into a glittering, candlelit Venetian palazzo. On one end of the enormous room was a wooden dance floor crowded with revelers in jewel-toned ball gowns and capes, elaborate feathered headdresses, and velvet masks. They twirled in time to a lively Renaissance tune played by the masked orchestra.

The scent of roses wafted towards them. Rita turned her gaze to the other end of the room, where the lunch tables had been covered in elegant white tablecloths, each one dotted with tea lights and with a vase of twelve red roses as a centerpiece. Beyond that, the ugly exposed brick walls had been covered by a gauzy backdrop of a Venetian canal, complete with palazzi and *gondolieri*.

Strands of little pink Christmas lights obscured the ceiling ducts, enveloping everyone in a warm rosy light.

"Isn't this the bees' knees?" her daughter-in-law Susan drawled.

"*Bellissimo*," Rita murmured in response, but her awe was tinged with trepidation. She was acutely aware that the clock was ticking down towards midnight and she was no closer to scrounging up dirt on her sister's blackmailer. All she had learned was that Viola hated Greta and quite possibly carried a torch for Orlando herself.

"Half of the town is here," Susan said as they descended the staircase. "At least I think so—I can't recognize anyone! Can you?"

Rita's dark eyes narrowed and swept the room as they came to the bottom of the stairs. She wagged her chin in the direction of a tall, spare man in a cheap-looking, obviously rented burgundy costume. "Father De La Pasqua," she said. "His Roman collar is showing."

Other than that, though, she had to admit she was stumped.

Rita was quite sure, however, that no one who spoke to Susan would fail to guess her identity, as she was the only person in town who sounded like a Southern version of Marilyn Monroe. And that was if her whippet-thin figure and slightly dim, deer-in-headlights expression—visible, Rita thought, even through Susan's rhinestone-studded black velvet mask—didn't give her away first. For the millionth time, Rita wondered why her beloved son had married a pale, twiggy, vegetarian

Southern Baptist. She could not understand why he had spurned the tried-and-true conventional wisdom that a man should marry a woman like his mother, and she took the fact that he had not as something of a personal affront.

Rita led her family over to the buffet table so that Sal and her two sons could set down the enormous platters of Rita's homemade desserts. Uncovering the platters, Rita gazed at her desserts as lovingly as she would have if they were her own three grown children.

For Susan's benefit, she pointed at the individual ramekins of what looked like deep, dark chocolate pudding. "*Sanguinaccio*," she said. Then she nodded towards the golden, cream-stuffed pastries next to them. "And *teste di turco*."

"*Sanguinaccio?*" Susan repeated faintly, clutching Marco's arm. "Doesn't that mean something like 'big blood?'"

"*Certo!* I must say, dear, those Italian lessons at the community college are really paying off."

"But that means...there's blood in it?"

"Traditionally, yes – it was made with chocolate and pigs' blood. Very rich, very delicious. A traditional Carnevale treat."

Marco put a hand on Susan's back, as if anticipating his vegetarian wife swooning into a faint.

"But"—Rita patted Susan on the arm—"this year, I caved to modern tastes and left the blood out."

"And the *teste di turco?*" Susan ventured timidly. "Doesn't that mean 'Turks' heads?'"

"*Certo!* The pastries are in the shape of turbans. Then you slice them in half, just like you're chopping the enemy's head off, and put a huge glob of whipped cream in the middle. I imagine they got their name during the era when Ottoman armies were ravaging Europe, or maybe during the Crusades, or even during the Arab conquest of Sicily. So many conflicts to choose from!"

Rita picked one up and took a delightful cream-filled bite, then patted the slightly green, open-mouthed Susan on the arm. "Oh, don't look so shocked, dear," she said. "We Italians may be bloodthirsty, but your ancestors started the Civil War."

Marco frowned, and Rita could almost see the words "now, Mother" forming on his lips. But, just in the nick of time, a woman in a teal ball gown studded with silver and gold beads suddenly bore down on them.

"Oh, thank God you're here!" said the woman, and Rita instantly recognized the voice as belonging to Bianca. Bianca had to shout over the deafening din, and she reached out to hug Gina. "I needed an excuse to get away from my dad and Greta. The PDA is absolutely revolting – they're like two teenagers in a backseat."

Rita raised her eyebrows as far as they could go.

"What I meant," Bianca said quickly, "was like *some* teenagers. Gina was never like that. She was practically a saint."

55

Rita rather doubted that, and her suspicions were confirmed by the glance that passed between Gina and Bianca.

Her youngest son Vinnie smiled, and his puppy dog brown eyes lit up. "Aw. I think it's sweet that even old people can find love."

"Old?" Bianca spat out the word, then frowned and stared out at the dance floor with sheer hatred. Rita followed her gaze. There was a man in a *medico delle peste* costume twirling a fair-haired maiden in an elaborate burgundy gown, bejeweled mask, and feathered headdress. If Rita was not mistaken, she'd seen that gown the day before. That couple had to be Orlando and Greta.

"Greta's forty-seven," Bianca said. "Closer to my age than my dad's."

"Only by a year, *cara*." Rita squeezed Bianca's shoulder. "I know it's hard to accept another woman into your father's life, but you'll always be the apple of his eye and, besides, doesn't he deserve some happiness after such an acrimonious divorce?"

Instead of answering the question, Bianca just sniffed, "Well, he won't find it with her. She's just a gold-digger." Bianca bit the top off a *testa di turco* with great ferocity, and Rita saw Susan flinch. "Sometimes," Bianca said, "I'd like to murder them both."

Then, suddenly bestowing a sweet smile on them all, Bianca said, "Your *teste di turco* are delicious as always, Mrs. C. It was so good seeing you all."

And with that, Bianca swept up Gina, and they headed across the dance floor, followed by Marco and Susan. Rita amused herself by looking at all the beautiful costumes. There were so many lovely bejeweled and embroidered gowns, wild feathered headdresses, and exotic masks; several bauta masks; and two *medici delle peste*.

Soon, Vinnie was dragged onto the dance floor by a flame-haired woman in a saffron-colored gown.

"You think she realizes it's Vinnie?" Sal chuckled. "Our Vinnie?"

Already halfway through his second *sanguinaccio*, Sal looked rather adorable with smudges of chocolate around his mouth.

Wiping the chocolate off his mouth, Rita gave him a kiss. "Our *figlio* is sweet, you know. And cute in a lost puppy-dog sort of way."

"Puppies," Sal grunted, "are a whole lot less work."

A petite woman in a gray ball gown and black-feathered headdress elbowed in between them and snatched a *sanguinaccio*. "I found you two at last."

The voice said it all: it was her sister, Rose.

"How'd you know it was us?"

"I've been circling the buffet table like a vulture for an hour now, waiting for someone to plunk down your desserts. I can spot your *sanguinaccio* from a mile away; all others are just poor imitations."

Rita basked in the compliment while Rose elbowed Sal in the ribs. "Why don't you get us two plates of lasagna?" she said. "And none of that vegetarian crap. Something really meaty, preferably with béchamel. Lidia Caravaggio's lasagna if there's any left."

Sal glowered at his sister-in-law. He did not like to be ordered around, least of all by the Mancini women.

"Can't you take a hint?" Rose said. "I need to talk girl talk with Rita."

Folding his massive forearms across his chest, Sal stalked away.

"So?" Rose asked once he had gone. "Did you get the dirt on Viola?"

"No. All I know is that she and Greta seem to be locked in a power struggle at the winery but, so far, Viola's winning. Plus, I'd guess she's in love with Orlando."

"You can't really blackmail her with that. I think half the town knows that."

"You know, blackmail *is* a crime. Why don't you just tell her you know she's blackmailing you and Greta and Orlando and threaten to go to the police?"

"Because," Rose hissed, "there'll be a trial. And then this will all come out, and I'll be in danger of losing my real estate license—or at least a lot of my clients. Plus, Paolo will be dragged through the mud."

"I thought things weren't serious between you two."

"That doesn't mean I want to cause him any trouble," Rose said stiffly.

Rita suppressed a smile. Clearly, Rose cared more for Paolo than she had let on.

"And besides," Rose added, "a trial would be terrible for Orlando and Greta, too. Who knows what they've done?"

Before Rita could even begin to speculate what those two might have done, Sal re-appeared, empty-handed. "*Mi dispiace*, but they're all out of lasagna at the moment. Now"—he bent down and kissed Rita's hand—"I hope this *bellissima* donna will do me the honor of the next dance."

With a giggle, Rita joined him on the dance floor, leaving Rose at the buffet. Rita wondered where Paolo was, or if Rose had even invited him.

"You really are light on your feet," Rita said, resting her head on Sal's chest with a contented sigh. "Like Fred Astaire."

"And you're my Ginger, *cara*," he murmured as he executed a turn, then pulled her in close against his stubbly cheek. "Remember when we would go to those school dances, then end up in the backseat of my tomato-red Pinto?"

"Oh, Sal!" She pretended to be scandalized, even though what had actually happened was not much of anything. She'd left plenty of space between them for the Holy Spirit, as Sister Helen had advised. However much he'd complained, Rita thought that Sal had secretly enjoyed the challenge.

A heavyset woman in deep purple bore down on them. "You-hoo! Rita! Rose pointed you out to me. You'll never guess—it's me, Marion!"

Rita smiled and pretended to be surprised, even though she could have guessed from the woman's girth alone. "What a lovely shade of purple," Rita said—which it was, although not on Marion. The dress made Marion resemble nothing quite so much as Barney the Dinosaur, which Rita had been forced to watch every afternoon when Vinnie was little.

"Are there any new developments with Matt Peruzzi and Gina?" Marion shouted. Her voice was so piercing that it actually cut through the roar of the crowd and caused several couples to swivel towards them, eager for the latest gossip.

Rita waited until they had turned away again before answering. "Nothing to report, I'm afraid. And now"— she looked heavenward, only to be blinded by the mass of pink Christmas lights—"it's out of my hands."

"Oh, that Lenten pledge," Marion clucked sympathetically. "You poor dear. Now that *is* a sacrifice."

As the song was coming to an end, Sal spun Rita and dipped her. Before Rita could get up, a glass shattered across the room. Then there was a loud thud and a collective gasp.

"Call a doctor!" someone yelled as someone else shouted, "It's Julia! Julia Simms."

Rita leapt up and craned her neck to see over the crowd. Had Julia Simms, the willowy, soft-spoken high school biology teacher, really collapsed? She seemed far too young for a heart attack and, in any case, she was one of those health-nut types who ate tofu and seaweed and ran five miles a day.

"Do you think she fainted?" Rita whispered to Sal. He shrugged. "It's pretty hot in here."

Mamma-bear pride surged through her as Marco and Susan dashed across the room. Marco looked suave and debonair in his black troubadour costume and black mask, which he hastily shoved up over his dark wavy hair. He was a doctor at the local hospital—an anesthesiologist, but a doctor nonetheless—and Susan was a nurse.

Rita dragged Sal, who was generally loath to be a rubbernecker, across the room. Then she left him on the periphery and dove under and through someone's legs until she had a clear view of poor Julia Simms, who was deathly pale and unresponsive, her flaxen hair arrayed out underneath her across the linoleum floor.

"You!" Marco shouted, pointing at a woman in a ruby red gown. "Call 9-1-1. Request an ambulance."

The terrified woman obeyed. Marco, usually so mild-mannered, was terrifically, thrillingly authoritative. He held up Julia's limp wrist and consulted his watch. "Pulse is forty and dropping," he murmured to Susan. Rita could tell from his tone that that was definitely not a good thing.

"Now," Marco said in a loud voice, "who saw what happened? Did she choke on something?"

Without waiting for an answer, though, Marco began poking around inside her mouth, checking for an obstruction. He came up empty-handed. Really, Rita thought, Marco could have a career recording first-aid videos. He was so much better than the horrible monotone third-rate actors they normally used.

"She just keeled over," one man said. He clutched the buffet table, clearly in shock. "Her wine glass hit the floor, and then she did."

"What was her condition before that?"

"She was slurring her words a bit. She seemed confused."

Marco nodded towards Susan. "Possible alcohol poisoning."

Rita shook her head. It was a sound medical diagnosis, she supposed, if one knew nothing of the person in question. But Julia Simms was hardly the type to get sozzled in a church basement.

The spilled wine was spreading slowly over the floor like a blood stain. Two women scurried over with a roll of paper towels and began sopping up the mess. After one of the women had soaked a dozen or more towels, she wadded them up and stood, and the crowd parted to make way.

"No!" Rita suddenly shouted. "Don't throw out the towels!"

Everyone turned to stare at her.

She pushed her mask up to her forehead. "These need to be entered into evidence."

A bewildered voice in the crowd said, "Evidence? Of what?"

"A crime."

With every eye upon her, Rita pushed her way through the throng of onlookers, ran into the kitchen, and emerged with a plastic garbage bag. Her humiliating days as a lunch lady—a job she took only so her children could get a tuition discount—had finally paid a dividend: she knew her way around the supply closet.

She pushed her way back through the crowd and held the bag open so the two astonished women could deposit their soggy purplish paper towels. Then Rita crouched down beside Miss Simms and, with the hem of her voluminous ball gown, picked up each shard of wine glass and placed it gently in the bag.

With a look of grim determination, she tied the handles together tightly. "You can never be too careful."

Chapter Nine

Rita knelt in a pew in the back of church, pinching herself to stay awake. It had been a long, sleepless night. By the time she'd handed her evidence to the police and filed her story ("Local Carnevale Celebrations End in Medical Emergency"), it had been after three o'clock—and then she'd been too keyed up to sleep a wink.

As the choir launched into some suitably somber dirge for Ash Wednesday, she snuck a glance at her phone. Marco had still not replied to her text asking for an update on Julia Simms' condition.

Father De La Pasqua had stepped off the altar and into the aisle. The congregants all rose and shuffled forward, single file, to receive their ashes. When it was Rita's turn, Father De La Pasqua plunged his thumb into the bowl and rolled it around and around. When he raised his hand, his thumb was completed covered in soot, blacker than black.

"Go and sin no more," he said in a loud voice, just as he had done for every other parishioner, as he made the sign of the cross on her forehead. She could feel the gritty ash seeping into her pores, and she had no doubt that her forehead now resembled a hot cross bun.

Then he winked and mouthed a private message just to her. "Remember, Rita—no meddling."

Rita tried to nod obediently, but she found herself rolling her eyes. Hmmm, she thought, hiding a smile, perhaps there's more of Gina in me—or me in her—than I thought.

When she returned to her pew, she prayed for Vinnie to finally, finally graduate from community college, Gina to find love and happiness with Matt Peruzzi, and Marco and Susan to hurry up and give her grandchildren.

She ended with a fervent prayer for Julia Simms' speedy recovery and then slipped out of church to go check on the patient herself.

Julia was awake and alert when Rita barged into her hospital room with a plate of biscotti and two steaming lattes.

"I know how horrible the cafeteria is," Rita said as she slid the biscotti onto Julia's lap and handed her a latte, "so I thought I'd bring some contraband. How are you, dear?"

"Fine, I think." Julia dipped her biscotti in the latte. Without her gold watch on, her wrist looked even bonier than usual, and for the first time, Rita noticed that she had a tiny butterfly tattoo. Julia patted her skinny thigh through her threadbare hospital gown. "Just a little sore where I hit the floor."

"Do you need me to go feed your cats?"

Julia gave Rita a grateful smile and nodded. "The key's under the mat."

"Consider it as good as done, dear—I'll even slip them some tuna tartare." Rita paused a moment and tried to look as if the next question had just suddenly popped into her head. "Did the doctors tell you anything about what might have caused you to collapse?"

"No. They're still running tests."

Rita wondered if that were really true, or if they were just baffled. Rita had a rather low opinion of most doctors—although that of course did not include her son Marco. "Well, do you remember anything before you lost consciousness? Did you eat or drink anything that tasted funny?"

Julia's big cornflower-blue eyes widened even further. With her pale face and flaxen hair spread out over the pillows, she reminded Rita of her childhood china doll. She had that perpetually innocent, almost startled look.

"Do you think I was...poisoned?"

"Not to alarm you dear, but forearmed is forewarned and yes, that's precisely what I think. It's very ironic, isn't it? The biology teacher with a Master's in botany, best known for her poison garden, is herself poisoned."

"*Former* poison garden. I tore up my garden after that horrible—incident. Now all I've got is petunias and begonias and tulips and daffodils."

"Now, don't blame yourself, dear. It was my article that put your poison garden on the map. Otherwise, Jay Stiglitz's murderer would never have known about it." Rita brushed a few crumbs off her blouse. "But even if your poison garden had never existed, Jay would have still been murdered. Where there's a will, there's a way!"

With a shudder, Julia said, "But who would want to murder me? And why? Rita, I have no stalkers, no jealous ex-boyfriends—"

"What about Frank, the one whose finger is fertilizing your garden?"

"Oh, no," Julia said, all wide-eyed innocence. "That was a mere kitchen mishap. We parted on the best of terms."

Rita did not see how one could be on good terms with someone to whom you'd lost a finger, but she decided it was best not to quibble. There was something a bit off about Julia Simms, anybody could see that, from her former obsession with growing a poison garden to her ghoulish decision to bury all her deceased cats there, not to mention poor Frank's finger. But killing her over a lost finger seemed rather extreme and, besides, it was rather a long time to wait for revenge.

"What about disgruntled students?" Rita asked.

"Oh, no. I'm such a softie that I never give anyone less than a 'B.' And I haven't sent anyone to detention in years."

"Jealous co-workers? You're department chair now, right?"

Julia shook her head. "Everyone seemed happy for me—and more than a little relieved. It's so much extra work, and yet the chair only gets paid an extra couple thousand dollars. Per hour, I probably make less than my students bussing tables at the Sunshine Café."

Rita frowned. Julia was not making this easy. "Family disputes? Trouble with neighbors? Someone standing to inherit a lot of money from you if you die?"

But Julia just kept shaking her head, steadfast in her belief that no one wished her ill and no one stood to gain from her death.

"Well, I give up," Rita said, throwing up her hands. "I've never met anyone who's a worse candidate to be murdered."

"Oh, well, I don't know about that. I don't think most people have anyone wanting to kill them."

Rita peered at Julia over her glasses, sighed, and patted her limp, pale hand. Julia was so trusting, so naïve. She had the air of an absentminded professor who was oblivious to the venality of human beings.

"You think that, dear," Rita said grimly, "but I can assure you that is not true. Why, I can think of a half dozen people who'd love to line up to murder me. The good news, of course, is that they'd never get away with it, and they know it, and they know I know it."

Julia tittered nervously. "Perhaps it was just too hot and I ate too much rich food—"

"You were white as a sheet, dear, and stone-cold unconscious."

"A case of mistaken identity, then. I was wearing a mask."

That much was true. Rita had only been able to identify Father De La Pasqua and Marion by sight, and Rose by her voice. Julia Simms had a tall, willowy figure and long blond hair. She was not sure that that alone would be enough to identify her in a room of several hundred. But her breathy voice – now that was rather distinctive. She sounded rather like Susan would if she ever lost the drawl and acquired a bland mid-Atlantic accent.

"Who did you speak to at the ball?"

"Father De La Pasqua, Greta Giroux, and Orlando Rinaldi," she said, ticking off each one on her fingers. "Paul Higgins, the chemistry teacher. I knew him by his scent alone—he smells like a chemistry lab. I danced with him a few times. Dr. Stevens, the new principal, and her husband."

"And no one said anything odd?"

"No. Paul talked about the new antidepressant he concocted for Piddles, his pet bunny. It seems to be working like a charm. And Dr. Stevens talked about her recent win in the Morris County tractor pull. And her husband was excited about a script he's writing for the Morris County Players. Apparently, it's an adaptation of *The Legend of Sleepy Hollow*, but set in outer space."

"Mmmm," Rita said, her voice thick with irony. "Nothing odd about any of that."

But as usual, all irony or sarcasm was lost on the innocent, always benevolent Julia Simms. Still, odd as it all was, nothing so much as hinted at a motive for murder.

"And you saw no one slipping anything in your drink?"

"No, although I can't say I was really watching it that carefully."

"And did anyone bring you food and drink?"

"Really, Rita, I'm sure it's nothing."

"I hope you're right, dear."

But Rita very much doubted it.

****

As Rita drove slowly home through the bleak, snowy landscape, she tried to cheer herself up by listening to an old Luciano Pavarotti CD. When even Luciano couldn't raise her spirits, she turned it off and drove in silence.

"Things have to look up," she said to herself out loud. "I mean, they can't get much worse."

But as she swung onto her street, she let out a groan. Parked in her driveway was a souped-up black truck with gold rims, a gold hood ornament, and a New Jersey vanity plate: VIT KING.

The self-proclaimed "vitamin king of Atlantic City," whom she suspected of peddling far more than just questionable supplements, was on her doorstep. She pulled in behind him, steeled herself for the inevitable, and then got out of the car, slamming the door loudly behind her.

"Rita!" he cried. Despite the cold, his coat was unzipped. A yellowed wifebeater, a thick carpet of salt-and-pepper chest hair, and several thick gold chains peeped out from under his open-necked shirt. "My favorite cousin's better half!"

"Calvino." She greeted him half-heartedly, attempting some sort of familial enthusiasm while wishing some other cousin was Calvino's favorite cousin—and that he was on his doorstep instead. With a hint of desperation, she said, "Ah, so you're just passing through on your way to visit your relatives in Boston, is it? How sweet of you to stop by."

"Naw," he said, "I've come to stay."

"Stay?" Rita clutched the doorknob for support, feeling as though her knees were about to give way. "Sal didn't tell me he'd invited you."

"Oh, he didn't. See, it was kinda a last-minute thing. Actually, I'm here to see you."

"Me? Whatever for?" She stared at him for a moment. "How's the family?" she asked suspiciously. "How's Concetta?"

"Well, er, that's the trouble—she kicked me out."

Rita felt her heart sink even lower. The last time Concetta had kicked him out and he'd come to stay, Calvino had sparked a house fire, eaten them out of house and home, and left a trail of cigar ash wherever he went.

"What did you do this time?"

"Nothing—I swear on my *mamma*'s grave, God rest her soul. Concetta just suddenly started reading some

71

crazy book about aliens and the next thing I know she's throwing pots and pans and saying she wants to be all 'self-actualized' or sumptin' like that. Rita, I don't even know what that means! I asked five guys and they were all like 'dude, never heard of it.' I mean, it's like you broads have some kinda secret language or sumptin'." Calvino shot her an aggrieved look, as though she were part of this female conspiracy to confuse men senseless. "Then next thing I know—bam!—she's chucking my clothes outta the bedroom window."

It took Rita a moment to translate this all in her head. Calvino always got everything all scrambled.

"You mean she was reading '*Men Are from Mars, Women Are from Venus*'?"

He snapped his fingers. "That's the one! I mean, how crazy is that? I ain't no astronaut. Anyways"—he brightened—"so then I thought, who's the smartest broad I know? Who can explain all this female mumbo-jumbo?" He thrust out an arm. "You!"

With a sigh, Rita opened the door and motioned him inside. It was going to be a very, very long Lent. If a visit from Calvino wasn't penance, she didn't know what was.

Chapter Ten

Rita plunked a steaming mug in front of Calvino, then went to check on the onions sautéing in her soup pot. Satisfied that they were sufficiently golden and translucent, she tossed in the spices and poured in the chicken stock.

"Self-actualized," she said, "means having a purpose in life."

Calvino shrugged. "She's got a purpose—taking care of me and the kids."

"Danielle and Frankie are grown up now. And you"—she took a large knife to a sweet potato and started chopping it furiously—"are a sixty-four-year-old man who should be capable of taking care of himself."

She scraped the diced sweet potatoes into the pot, imagining that her blade was sliding across Calvino's neck rather than her cutting board.

"Notice," she said, "I said 'should.' And have you considered that maybe Concetta wants you to take care of her for a change?"

"I took her to Olive Garden a few weeks ago."

"Sure, but do you support her dreams, her aspirations?"

"She plays bridge and does water aerobics. We spend a whole week in Florida every winter at a place so fancy they've got these special pool towels and a coffeemaker in the room."

Rita caught herself rolling her eyes. Maybe Gina had gotten that from her after all.

"She's got two grandbabies," he said. "What more does she want?"

"Well, did you ask her?"

"Ask her what?"

"What she wants."

"No." He crossed his massive arms over this chest and glared at Rita. "And I'm not gonna. She's gonna have to come groveling back to me."

"And until then?"

"I'm staying right here."

Rita turned on her stick blender to puree the soup— and to cover up the string of Italian cusswords she was muttering under her breath. Rita abhorred swearing, so this was just one indication of how dire the situation was. She had to get Concetta to take Calvino back—and soon.

She poured him a bowl of soup and set it down with a clatter. Then she cut a slice of crusty Italian bread and plunked it down next to the bowl. "*Mangia!*"

"What?" he said. "No butter? No meat?"

"It's Ash Wednesday," she hissed, pointing at the giant black smudge on her forehead. Calvino's forehead, though gouged with deep wrinkles, had no such mark. "A day of fasting. A day of penance."

74

Silently, she added, "Which is the only reason I'm putting up with you."

Then she sailed through the swinging door to the dining room and hit the speed dial button for Father De La Pasqua.

"*Padre*," she gasped, "I hate to interrupt you, but this is an emergency. Sal's shady cousin from Jersey just showed up. I need a dispensation from my Lenten resolution so that I can call his wife and patch things up between them. I beg you, *Padre*. It's in everyone's best interest."

"But is it, Rita?" He had that infuriating father-knows-best tone. It was easy for him to say—he'd never had Calvino on his doorstep. "After all," Father De La Pasqua went on, "you've meddled, er, intervened before, and where did that get you? He's right back on your doorstep. Maybe you need to let them work out their own problems this time."

"But that could take weeks—years!"

"Have faith, Rita, and look for a silver lining. I'm sure things will work out. Now I really must go. I'm late for a meeting of the church decorating committee."

Rita thought of the committee co-chairs and winced.

"You see?" Father De La Pasqua said, as if reading her mind. "We all have our trials."

Chapter Eleven

A late February thaw melted most of the snow, and Spring was most definitely in the air by the day of the foraging expedition. As she tramped through the sun-dappled woods, her coat unbuttoned in defiance of Old Man Winter, Rita felt her spirits soar. It was one of those days that reminded her how blessed she was to call the Hudson Valley home.

It was so splendid, in fact, that she could almost forget that her boorish Neanderthal of a houseguest was just a few paces behind her, laden down with Rocco's camera and tripod. Rocco was laid low with the flu and Calvino, whatever his faults, was a decent amateur photographer, so Rita had decided that the least Calvino could do was to make himself useful. Plus, past experience had taught her not to leave him unsupervised for more than a few hours.

Viola looked radiantly happy, too, but this was perhaps not surprising. As the leader of their little expedition, she was in her element. She set the rules, she told them what to touch and what not to, where to look for what plant, and how to prepare it. It was as though she were hall monitor again—except the consequence of ignoring her dictums was not a demerit, but a slow and painful death.

"We're like her twelve disciples," Rita murmured to Rose as she counted the members of their little party.

"Disciples? She's more like the anti-Christ." Narrowing her eyes, Rose added, "There are thirteen of us. How horribly unlucky."

Rita felt her pulse quicken. She didn't want anything to happen to anyone, of course, not really—but it would make a good story.

"Sam is hoping," she joked, "that we'll trip over a body in the woods."

"Well, if someone's got to die," Rose muttered, "I certainly hope it's Viola."

Rita stifled a giggle. "You shouldn't say that, Rose. Although, I must say, you don't seem to be the only one struggling with murderous impulses."

She tilted her head in the direction of Bianca, who trailed behind her completely lovestruck father and soon-to-be stepmom. Judging by the frequent glares she sent their way, her antipathy towards Greta seemed to be accelerating as the wedding approached. The objects of her hatred seemed completely oblivious, however, as they walked hand in hand and often cheek to cheek through the forest. Whenever Viola pointed out a plant, they gave it the briefest of glances before resuming their Eskimo kisses and whispered sweet nothings.

"I think Bianca's dead wrong," Rita said with a sigh. "The money may be a perk, but Greta's no gold digger. I think she's truly in love with Orlando."

"Or she's a really good actress. Although he is certainly a good catch. Good-looking, smart, successful, cultured—and he comes with all of the wine you can drink!"

Rita smiled, remembering how Rose had once tried to reel Orlando in, but he had proved rather impervious to her sister's considerable charms. Rose might be good-looking for her age, but Greta was twenty years younger. So, as cultured as Orlando was, perhaps he wasn't that different from other men after all.

"And she's not the only member of our party nursing a grudge," Rita said. She waggled her chin in the direction of McKenzie Reagan, a mousy little slip of a girl who was trudging alongside her boyfriend, Luca Della Rosa. Luca had recently put Morris County on the map with its first Michelin star. A thirty-something, devastatingly handsome graduate of the Culinary Institute of America, he was the owner of a nose-to-tail high-end butcher shop and the kind of upscale farm-to-table restaurant that Sal derided for "gerbil-sized portions" and "weird-ass, newfangled foods like calf's brains with sea foam." Sal was convinced that Luca's restaurant was going to be the epicenter of the next mad cow disease epidemic, although Sal sometimes floated an alternate theory that the patrons had already contracted mad cow disease, and that's why they were willing to pay through the nose for snooty service and skimpy portions.

Rita lowered her voice. "In the parking lot, I overheard McKenzie say, 'I should have known she'd be here.'"

"She, who?" Rose said.

"I think she meant Greta. She was staring at Greta as she said it, and not in a nice way at all."

"What could she have against Greta?"

"Who knows? Maybe she's just a loyal friend of Bianca's. I haven't seen them together much, but they are about the same age."

Calvino caught up to them just then, flushed and out of breath. "I guess I need to spend more time pumping iron. This tripod's heavy." He winked. "It's not all bad bringing up the rear, though. I get a nice view of some tail."

Rita followed his gaze to three, tall, slender women in expensive ski jackets, tight jeans, and knee-high leather boots.

"I hope," she said icily, "you are referring to some squirrels or perhaps white-tailed deer. It is not polite, Calvino, to objectify women."

Calvino looked genuinely hurt. "Wazza matter with appreciating beauty?"

"It's too forward, Calvino. Too sexual."

"So what should I say?"

"Nothing—and don't let your eyes do the talking, either."

"So, what? I'm supposed to walk around with my eyes shut and my lips zipped?"

"Yes, if possible. If you really must look at a woman, keep your eyes above neck level. If you must comment on a woman's appearance, compliment her hair or her outfit. And try focusing more on her other traits, like her intelligence. Ask her about her job, her family, or her hobbies."

Calvino hung his head. "That's a lot for a fella to remember. You women are so complicated. All these secret rules. Is this what they taught you when they separated us in sixth grade?"

"No, Calvino, that was the hygiene lecture."

Calvino shot a glance at Rose, who looked quite amused. "Rita's teaching me the rules, see? Like how to talk to women and help them be all 'self-actualized.'" He frowned, as if trying to remember something. "Oh, yeah—I like your coat, Rose. And your hair. It's real shiny."

Rita smiled at him encouragingly.

"I like your coat, too, Rita. And hers—what's her name?"

He was back to staring longingly at the three younger women.

"Aria Champlain," Rita said with a sigh. She supposed he was trying.

"Is she the leader of the pack?"

"How'd you know?"

"I dunno. I guess how she carries herself, like she's real important." He wagged his chin at the other two. "And who are her little mini-mes?"

"The redhead's Diana Cotesworth-Beddington. She's a stay-at-home mom of three. And Teri Bertinelli. She and her husband own the farm next to the winery and have two kids. The land's been in her family for three generations."

"Guess she's not too happy about the winery expansion," Calvino said, then blushed. "Okay, okay—I looked at her rack. I mean, you don't put a huge pin on your chest unless you want people to look."

Rita had to concede that, for once, Calvino was right. All three women had enormous pins on their chests with a big "X" though the words "winery expansion." When Calvino had taken a group picture in the parking lot, it had been amusing to watch the three battle with Orlando, Greta, and Viola to see who would get in the front. In the end, the three had elbowed them out just as Calvino snapped the picture, ensuring that the buttons made the front page of the *Morris County Gazette*.

Beautiful, blonde Aria Champlain was indeed the ringleader. President of the PTA and the local Democratic party, yoga instructor, marathoner, and self-styled lifestyle guru, she lived for the limelight and was supremely good at filling it. Diana and Teri were her most dedicated acolytes, although there were at least a dozen other thirtysomething moms in her orbit. Rita wasn't sure if Aria was passionately opposed to the winery expansion for its own sake, or just because she needed another cause to champion. Teri had a personal stake in the outcome, too, given that her family's land abutted the winery—plus, she might have a more personal vendetta; her aunt was Orlando's ex-wife Marie, who liked to claim that she had been cheated out of her fair share of the winery during their acrimonious divorce. Rita rather doubted this, however, as Marie seemed to still be living the life to which she had become accustomed, shuttling between her Florida home, her Morris County retreat, her Manhattan apartment, and endless trips to the spa and the tanning salon in her black limo. And Diana—well, Diana just did whatever Aria wanted; she seemed content to bask in Aria's reflected glow.

"And who's the Boy Scout?" Calvino asked.

"Jack. He's a new employee at the winery."

"Doesn't seem the sharpest tool in the shed, does he?"

Rita let the comment slide, although she secretly agreed. They continued on in companionable silence, following Viola's jaunty beret as if it were a beacon, up and down hillsides, past mushroom-sprouting logs, beside bogs choked with weeds (some of which, to Rita's surprise, were edible), and through valleys of ferns.

"Now these," Viola said as she reached out and cut a fern at its base, "are delicious steamed or sautéed in a light sauce."

Rita jotted that down while motioning for Calvino to get a close-up. Then she leaned down, snipped several stalks, and threw a bunch of fiddleheads into her basket, while everyone else did the same.

They came to the edge of a swampy area, and Viola pointed to a tall weed that looked like Queen Anne's lace, with a long slender stalk culminating in a pom-pom of little delicate white buds.

"Now, come closer," Viola said, "because this is very important. The stem makes all the difference. If you see a plant like this with a mottled stem like this"—she ran a gloved hand within an inch of the stem—"it's water hemlock, one of the most poisonous plants that grow in this area. Many people call the roots 'dead man's fingers,' since it's where the poison is most concentrated. An amount just the size of the tip of your thumb is enough to kill someone."

Greta shuddered. "How terrible. Viola can't you show us something...nicer? Something we can actually eat?"

Viola shot her younger rival an icy smile. "Ignorance is bliss, but it can also kill you. I'm showing this to everyone so you don't pick it—and so you can distinguish it from the very delicious wild carrot, which looks almost identical, but doesn't have a mottled stem. Now"—she shot a pointed glance at Greta—"if you'll come this way, I'll show you wild carrots, which I trust will meet with your approval as a 'nice' plant. They aren't quite as sweet as domesticated carrots, but they're wonderfully flavorful. Perhaps a bit much for a salad, but excellent when cooked."

As Viola led them to a clump of nearly identical-looking plants nearby, Rose muttered "score one for Viola" just loud enough for Rita to hear.

Forty-five minutes later, after a few more pointers and stern warnings, Viola set them loose to forage for their supper.

As she snipped, plucked, and gathered, Rita kept her ears pricked for Calvino's attempts at polite conversation with the women of the party. He was earnestly trying to put into practice her lessons, sometimes with comic results.

"You got real pretty hair," he said to Bianca as they gathered wild garlic. "Real shiny. How do you get it like that?"

"Uh, shampoo," was Bianca's laconic reply.

"So how do you, uh, 'self-actualize' yourself? Like are you one of those smarty-pants types who reads a lot? Or you got kids?"

"Nope," Bianca said. Rita noticed that Bianca's eyes drifted to Luca as she said this. "I'm not married."

Calvino chucked a wild garlic bulb into his basket. "So your dad's getting married, huh?"

"Not if I can help it," Bianca muttered before hastily excusing herself to go look for some ramps.

Soon, McKenzie had inadvertently wandered into the path of Calvino's charm offensive.

"So, you got a job?" he said as an ice-breaker. Rita noticed he was staring resolutely, almost unnervingly, at McKenzie's chin. He had taken Rita's instructions a little too literally.

McKenzie smiled at him, and two dimples appeared on her cheeks. "I'm a chef," she said proudly, "at the Sunshine Café."

"Wow! I've eaten there, you know. The food's real good. I won the two-pound burger challenge," he said proudly. "Twice."

"Oh, yeah, I remember seeing your picture on the wall."

"I also like the desserts," he said. "Specially the apple pie cheesecake."

"That's my recipe."

"No kiddin'. Well, in that case"—he winked at her—"you're gonna be formidable competition in the cooking contest later today."

"Yeah, well, my cooking's nothing compared to Luca's. But I'll just be happy to have him win. At least, I think he'll win—his only real competition is Rita and maybe Bianca."

"Oh, yeah?"

"Bianca's the pastry chef at the winery. She makes a mean puff pastry, and her pots de creme are legendary. Just because she can bake doesn't mean she can cook, though."

"What about Greta?" Calvino asked. "Does she cook?"

"I doubt it." McKenzie's voice was suddenly frosty. "Unless you count ordering the real cooks around. She excels at ordering other people around. She thinks she's so perfect, you know? It's infuriating."

Calvino jerked a thumb in Viola's direction. "Even more than Miss Know-it-All?"

McKenzie suddenly laughed. "Those two," she said, "deserve each other."

Rita was itching to hear what else McKenzie knew about Viola—especially if it was something that could help Rose—but before McKenzie could say any more, they were interrupted by a shriek from somewhere down the hillside.

Rita, Calvino, and McKenzie scrambled down the hill to the edge of the pond, where a dark-haired head bobbed up and down and two purple-clad arms thrashed in the icy waters, struggling for purchase on the thin coating of ice that pulsed above the water. "It's Bianca!" Rita shouted. "She's fallen through the ice!"

Rita had always regarded Bianca as a levelheaded young woman, so she could not imagine what would possess her to set off across the ice on an unseasonably warm day. Bianca had to have suspected that the surface was not solid.

Orlando ran to and fro, searching for a large stick to extend out to where Bianca had fallen in, and Rita did likewise. She was under no illusion that the ice would hold her considerable weight, if it hadn't held slim Bianca's.

"I'm calling 9-1-1!" she heard Jack shout from somewhere behind her.

"They'll never get here in time," Greta wailed. "Someone, do something!"

To Rita's surprise, that someone turned out to be Calvino. Lickety-split, he leapt onto the frozen surface, immediately falling through, then thrashing his way towards Bianca. The ice fell all around him, and soon he had her tucked securely under one beefy arm and was dragging her to shore.

The party erupted into cheers and then McKenzie and Greta swiftly dragged her behind a bush. A minute later, Bianca emerged, dazed and shivering, in McKenzie's coat and Greta's pants. Greta was barefoot and barelegged, but was wearing a long coat—overkill in this weather, Rita had thought, but now it seemed a godsend—that went down to her knees.

Calvino handed his camera to Rita and his tripod to Orlando. Then he hoisted Bianca up and began running up the trail. By the time the party straggled into the parking lot, Calvino had Bianca in Rita's car with the heat on full blast.

"Calvino," Rita said, giving him a hug, "you've done me proud."

Chapter Twelve

An hour later, after Bianca and Calvino had changed clothes and warmed up beside the winery's roaring fire, the eleven contestants stood behind their cook stations, listening intently to Viola's instructions. Bianca had made a quick recovery from her dip in the pond and was behind her cook station, which was sandwiched between Orlando's and Greta's. Calvino also seemed unfazed by his brush with hypothermia, but given that he had never cooked a day in his life, going right from enjoying his *mamma*'s cooking to his wife's, and that he was needed to photograph the proceedings, he was not competing. Instead, he roamed the floor, snapping candid photos.

"You've got two hours," Viola said to the contestants, "to make an appetizer, a main course, and a dessert, and each course must prominently feature at least one foraged food from your basket. You get extra credit if you can incorporate multiple foraged foods in each dish. And remember"—she admonished them with a wag of her finger—"wild foods taste a bit different than their domesticated counterparts, so it's important to taste your dishes as you go. You may need to adjust quantities or seasonings."

She set the timer, and the frenzy began. Each contestant crammed into the pantry, sharp elbows out, to frantically gather the other ingredients they might need.

For the first course, Rita had decided on stinging nettle soup. Since the recipe she'd found online called for potatoes and shallots, she decided to earn bonus points by substituting burdock, which supposedly tasted like a blend of potatoes and artichokes, and ramps, much beloved by foodies and reminiscent of shallots and garlic.

The entrée was a bit trickier, but when she saw the filets of turbot in the refrigerator, she knew that a seafood dish was the way to go. She'd flavor the fish with ramp butter, plate it over lemony sautéed sheep sorrel, and top the fish with a hollandaise sauce flavored with goutweed (a traditional treatment for gout, the weed apparently tasted like a cross between parsley, celery, and carrots). For a side dish, she'd whip up a risotto with wild oyster mushrooms.

The only vaguely dessert-like ingredients she had gathered were wild carrots, so carrot cake seemed like the obvious, if not very creative, choice. But she'd need to increase the sugar to compensate for the lower sugar content, and the cake would be white, not a lovely orange.

Rushing back to her kitchen station laden down with armfuls of chicken stock, heavy cream, fish, eggs, and baking ingredients, Rita set a pot of salted water on the stovetop, and began grating the carrots for the cake.

Then she slid on her gloves and blanched the stinging nettles, removing their sting, by tossing them in the pot of boiling water and then in an ice bath.

Calvino came up behind her, snapping away. "Let's get an action shot, Rita. Something dramatic."

With a flourish, she tossed the minced ramps into a sizzling wok of olive oil and butter. "Is that dramatic enough for you?"

"Perfect."

As he took a few close-ups of the vegetables and herbs she had prepped, Calvino leaned closer and murmured, "Wanna know what the competition is cooking up?"

In spite of herself, Rita had to admit she did. It was billed as a friendly competition, and she was of course covering the event for the paper, but she wanted to win—badly. As the fourteen-time champion of the St. Vincent's pasta-making contest, she had a reputation to uphold. And if she could best the only resident of Morris County with a Michelin star, well that would be just one more feather in her cap.

"Spill it, Calvino."

He told her what everyone was cooking, but she mostly paid attention to his intel on her only real competition: Bianca and Luca.

"Bianca's doing some kinda fancy-schmanzy chicken pot pie," he said, "only with burdock, ramps, and wild carrots instead of potatoes, onions, and regular carrots."

That certainly made sense, given Bianca's mastery of puff pastry. She was cleverly playing to her strengths.

"What about her first course and dessert?"

"A salad with daylily shoots and carrot cake."

Rita frowned. Bianca's carrot cake might give hers a run for its money.

"What's she putting in the carrot cake?"

"Walnuts, I think. That's the only ingredient I see besides flour and stuff like that."

Rita made a mental note to jazz hers up with some canned pineapple. She had spotted a can in the corner of the pantry.

"And Luca? What's our Michelin-starred chef cooking up?"

"Steak with mashed burdock and wild parsnips, grilled ramps, and a sauce with garlic mustard greens."

Rita remembered that Viola had said that the taproots tasted like horseradish. That certainly would go well with steak. Still, she didn't think it was the most creative dish.

"And for a starter," Calvino said, "penne pasta with ramp pesto and *guanciale*."

Guanciale was pork cheek, and it featured prominently on upscale Italian menus.

"Dessert?"

"A flourless chocolate cake with wild Kentucky coffee beans."

Rita's heart sank. She should have thought of that. She was a pasta champion and made a renowned flourless chocolate cake. Luca was encroaching on her territory.

As if reading her mind, Calvino winked. "*Non ti preocupare.* You're gonna win. I spiked his flourless chocolate cake batter with goutweed when he wasn't looking."

"Calvino!"

Rita tried to look indignant, but she found it hard not to laugh.

"You can thank me later," he said.

As Rita added chopped burdock, chicken stock, bay leaves, and thyme to the pot, and began dredging the fish in egg wash and Italian bread crumbs, Calvino went over to Rose's station, where she was cooking a rather unimaginative dinner (a salad of raw greens and a roasted chicken with roasted burdock) in a desultory fashion. Clearly, Rose was not in it to win it.

"What's for dessert?" Rita asked, looking over at her sister.

"Nothing," Rose said tartly. "My theme is 'Weight Watchers.'"

"Very clever."

Rita sauntered over to her twin's station and lowered her voice. Calvino had already moved on to photograph Greta's station, where she appeared to be making some kind of carrot soup.

"You know, sis, if you have a bladder infection, you should try cranberry juice."

"Bladder infection?" Rose looked affronted. "What do you think I am—some doddering old lady? I most certainly do *not* have a bladder infection."

"But you keep leaving your station to go to the ladies' room."

"I keep leaving my station to do reconnaissance."

"On what?"

"On Viola."

"Really? And what have you learned?"

"That the staff hate her, that she's in love with Orlando but he has no idea, and that she hates Greta.

She and Bianca spend quite a lot of time together these days, *pettegolando* about Greta."

Rita looked over at Greta, who was leaning earnestly over her cook stove and slurping a bit of soup off of a wooden spoon. Greta frowned and added another dash of salt.

"*Poverina,*" Rita muttered.

Other than Orlando, Greta hadn't a friend in the world.

Chapter Thirteen

The clock was ticking down towards the deadline. Rita had ladled her velvety, green, steaming hot soup into individual bowls and plated her turbot with the sheep sorrel and creamy wild mushroom risotto. Now she had only to frost the carrot cake.

She placed one round cake layer on a platter, then spread a thick cream cheese frosting on top. She could hear the whirring of electric beaters, the slamming of oven doors, and the excited babble of her fellow contestants. But it all faded into the background. She was concentrating on only one thing—winning the competition.

Picking up the second cake pan, she ran a knife around the edge and quickly inverted it on a plate. Just as she was gingerly sliding it on top of the first frosted layer, a voice behind her made her jump.

"Rita."

Startled, she let the cake layer slip out of her fingers, and the warm cake landed with a thud slightly off center. A spider web of little cracks spread over the surface.

She spun around, scowling. "Couldn't you have—?"

The words died on her lips. She was face to face with Orlando Rinaldi, who was white as a sheet and wringing his hands anxiously.

"Rita," he said, "I need you to come with me. Now."

Orlando led Rita into his office and shut the door. The moment they were alone, his shoulders slumped.

"She's on the sofa," he said in a hoarse whisper.

The sofa was facing the fireplace, flanked by two wing chairs. From the door, Rita could see nothing but its plush velvet back.

"She said she felt dizzy," Orlando said as Rita crept across the room. "Said she needed to lie down. I didn't think anything of it, just thought she was tired after a long day and all the drama with Bianca."

Orlando burst into a sob just as Rita peeked over the side of the sofa and caught a glimpse of Greta's beautiful face, twisted in pain, turquoise eyes wide open, unseeing.

"Oh, Orlando," Rita murmured, tears pricking at her eyes. "She's beyond any help I can offer. Mi dispiace."

"Can you just—make sure?"

With a sigh, Rita lifted one of Greta's pale, limp wrists. It was still warm, but there was no pulse. She held it longer than necessary, then tried the other wrist just to be sure. "Mi dispiace," she said again, in a low but firm voice. "È morta."

As Rita was setting Greta's arm back down, a tiny blue object caught her eye. She twisted Greta's wrist around and stared.

Motioning for Orlando to come closer, she pointed at the inside of Greta's wrist. "What's this?"

Keeping his eyes averted from the rest of his fiancée's body, as if looking at her would cause excruciating pain, he said, "Her butterfly tattoo."

"How long has she had this?"

"I don't know. As long as I've known her—why?"

"Because," she said slowly, "Julia Simms has the exact same tattoo."

Rita left Orlando in his office and hurried back to the kitchen, acutely aware that the sheriff would be barreling through the door in less than twenty minutes. She had mixed feelings about the fact that the murder had occurred outside Acorn Hollow's city limits. On the one hand, she wouldn't have a back channel to the investigation through her friend Detective Benedetto—the only detective in Morris County worth his salt. But on the other, she was sure to play the starring role in solving the case. There was no way Sheriff D'Onofrio was going to piece this one together.

Rita rummaged through her purse, found a luridly pink plastic bag—the kind she used to pick up what Acorn Hollow quaintly termed "pet waste"—and slid it over her hand as a makeshift plastic glove. Then, she crossed quickly to Greta's workstation and poked and prodded her way through the wastebasket that lay beside it. It took only a minute to make the grim discovery she had half-expected, half-feared: a mottled stem. She looked around to make sure no one was watching, then used her phone to snap several photos before crossing over to Aria Champlain's station, where Calvino was earnestly photographing her wild mushrooms on toast, pad Thai incorporating ramps, and carrot cake. Rita felt a ripple of schadenfreude as she took in Aria's cake, which had a huge crater on top and looked about as light and airy as a six-month-old fruitcake.

"I usually just do Blue Apron," Aria was saying, looking slightly chagrined as she poked the top of the cake with one long, bedazzled finger. The diamond on her engagement ring was as big as a grape.

"Huh." Calvino clearly had no idea what she was talking about. "So that's, er, one of your hobbies? What other hobbies do you have? Like, are you in a bowling league?"

Aria looked completely aghast. Rita bet anything she was trying to picture herself in one of those hideous, baggy bowling shirts.

"Calvino," Rita trilled, "I hate to interrupt, but I need you."

She led him away from Aria and her groupies and whispered in his ear, "Do not let anyone remove anything from Greta's workstation—I mean anything. And don't under any circumstance let anyone sample anything she made either."

Calvino shot her a questioning look, but when no explanation was forthcoming, he just shrugged and took up his place by Greta's station. He was, Rita reflected with a twinge of affection, rather like a loyal and obedient, if not very bright, lap dog. Perhaps that's what Concetta had seen in him—at least, until she caught the self-actualization bug.

Just then, the buzzer rang, and Viola clapped her hands delightedly.

"And time!" Viola shouted.

Out of the corner of her eye, Rita saw the door open and the sheriff and his deputies enter.

"Yes, it is time," Rita said with a nod to the approaching deputies, as a few contestants gasped, "but not for judging the contest. It's time to begin a murder investigation."

Chapter Fourteen

While his deputies photographed and bagged the contents of Greta's workstation, and removed her body from Orlando's study, Sheriff D'Onofrio took Rita's statement. They faced each other over a rustic wooden table in the far corner of the tasting room, out of earshot of the others.

Sheriff D'Onofrio was glaring at Rita. His massive shoulders were hunched up; his thick neck was sunk down. "Murder?" he growled, repeating her earlier words. "Who said anything about murder? This is the initial investigation of a suspicious death, no more, no less. It could very well turn out to be an accident."

"In my experience," Rita said archly, "women with this many enemies never die in accidents."

With a roll of his eyes and a weary sigh, he opened his notebook and clicked his pen. "And I bet you're all ready to tell me about these enemies."

"*Certo!*" Rita brightened and launched into a detailed explanation of Aria's crusade against the winery expansion, Teri's more self-interested opposition to the winery expansion as a neighboring property owner and Orlando's ex-wife's niece, and Diana's dogged devotion to Aria and her latest crusade.

Sheriff D'Onofrio seemed unimpressed. "They're just bored housewives," he said with a dismissive wave of his hairy, stub-fingered hand, "not killers. Now, Bianca, though—I heard a rumor that she said she wanted to kill Greta."

For once, he was not wrong, but it would be cruel to admit this. Images of Bianca and Gina flitted through Rita's mind; she thought of the time they'd caused quite a stir strutting down the street in Rita's high heels and old bridesmaid's dresses, the hems trailing in the puddles, the bodices pooling around their teeny seven-year-old waists. Or the time Bianca and Gina had "run away" together, used all their money in their piggy banks to buy two Happy Meals, and then called Rita to pick them up two hours later. Or the time they'd adopted a baby bunny rabbit and smuggled it into school in Bianca's backpack.

"If she said it," Rita sniffed, "it was only a figure of speech. I've known her since she was three; that girl wouldn't hurt a lamb."

As she said this, though, her mouth suddenly felt very dry. Her hand shook as she reached for her water glass. Luckily, the sheriff did not seem to notice. But then he didn't notice much. That's why she'd solved the last murder in Morris County—and why she'd have to solve this one, too.

"And what about Orlando?" he said. "I'm not saying it's murder—in fact, I'm almost sure it's not—but if it were...well, it's usually the husband."

"Oh, no—Orlando would never do something like that, first of all, because he's a stand-up guy, and, second, because he loves—loved—her. Anyone can see that."

The sheriff grunted. "Did you know if he had a lover—or she did?"

"*Certo che non!*"

Even as she said this, though, she remembered that both Greta and Orlando were being blackmailed by Viola. She wondered just what Viola knew. Could Greta have been having an affair?

"At least," Rita conceded, "I can't imagine Orlando having an affair. I doubt Greta was either, but I can't say I knew her well at all. I had maybe three or four short conversations with her." Rita hesitated, then leaned forward and said. "I think you need to take a closer look at Viola."

At this, his big glowering dark eyes nearly popped out of his head.

"She's in love with Orlando," Rita said, "and she resents Greta terribly, both as a rival for Orlando's affections—and her hold on the business. Plus"—she flushed—"she is—was—blackmailing Greta."

"And how would you know that?"

Rita's heart sank. If she told the truth, her sister would never speak to her again. So instead she told a lie that no one—no one living at least—could contradict. "Greta told me."

"The same Greta that you hardly knew?"

Rita frowned. Sometimes Sheriff D'Onofrio showed a glimmer of intelligence, and always at the most inconvenient times.

"That's what made it so surprising, Sheriff—that she confided in me, that is."

"And when was this?"

"Today, on the hike. You see, she was acting very strangely around Viola and so I asked her what was wrong."

"And she just blurted it out?"

"Oh, well...." Rita said vaguely, stalling for time. But then she remembered that the sheriff had more than a little in common with her boorish houseguest. "You know how women are," she said. "So emotional."

His response told her that her gambit had worked.

"Mmmm, yes," he muttered, no doubt thinking of his wife's or daughter's latest outburst. "Unfortunately, I do."

The next morning, Rita let out a deep sigh as she took her first sip of her morning espresso and plopped down into a chair at her kitchen table. She had not told Sheriff D'Onofrio about Julia's and Greta's matching tattoos. Was that wrong—or just a natural result of her principled refusal to meddle?

After all, there was no definitive linkage between the two, and he'd probably have pooh-poohed her whole theory anyway. Plus, he hadn't asked. Of course, he hadn't asked if Viola was blackmailing Greta either, and that hadn't stopped her from blurting that out.

Doing the right thing, Rita thought, was hard enough; knowing what was the right thing was sometimes even harder.

Another loud sigh from Rita caused Calvino to look up from the newspaper and grin. "You're not looking so hot this morning, Rita."

"Neither are you," she grunted, taking in his matted hair, five o'clock shadow, and bleary dark eyes, "and I at least have a good excuse. I stayed up until four in the morning to finish my story."

"Yeah, that was some doozy of a story." He flipped to the front page and tapped the headline 'Foraging Trip Ends in Tragedy' with a fat, chocolate-smudged thumb while munching happily on one of her homemade peanut butter biscotti. Calvino always ate with his mouth gaping open, and today was no exception. Biscotti crumbs were flying everywhere, and Luciano and Cesare crouched beside him, racing each other for each morsel that rained down on them like manna from heaven. "So does that make you feel all, uh, self-actualized? Writing about some chick choking on poisonous weeds? Staying up all night and looking like death warmed over?"

"Under the circumstances," Rita said, pointed accusingly at him with her biscotti, "that's a very poor choice of words, Calvino. And here's a tip—never tell a woman she looks terrible in the morning. All women like to think that they look their best at their most natural, first thing in the morning."

"Well, if they think they look so great in the morning, then why do they bother with make-up?"

"Because—oh, well, never mind."

The truth was that Rita didn't have a good answer to his question. It reminded her of the time Gina, at age three, had asked her why Jesus's father was part of the trinity, but not his mother, and Rita, flummoxed and ill-equipped to answer even after years of catechism, had sputtered that she would tell Gina when she was older. The trick, when dealing with men or children, was to act as if the concept was either so self-evident or so complicated that one could not be bothered to explain it.

"It's not the death and destruction, or the stress or the hours that make me feel self-actualized," she said. "It's feeling like I'm doing an important service to the community. Keeping them informed, building community spirit."

"Yeah, some community spirit you got here—the community comes together, and one chick almost drowns and another gets poisoned." He took another big bite of biscotti. "So you think Concetta wants to, um, be like a journalist or community organizer or sumptin' like that?"

"No, Calvino." Rita tried not to choke on her biscotti. The only things Concetta read were her horoscope, celebrity gossip, and fashion magazines. "Probably more like go to beauty school." But then she remembered her pledge. "Or become an astronaut. I mean, what do I know? Really, you should just ask her yourself."

"See, that's the thing." Calvino was looking sheepish now. "I was thinking maybe you could ask her. You know, have one of those girl talks. And then you could tell me what I need to do."

"I can't. My *fioretto* is not to intervene in the lives of others—well, except to solve a murder."

Calvino stared at her, then jiggled his earlobes as if he literally could not believe his ears. "Whose harebrained idea was that?"

"Gina's."

He grunted. "Well, she's not the only one giving terrible advice around here." He flipped to page five and tapped the rightmost column. "Check this out. 'Dear Dude'," he read, " 'I've had a crush on this guy for years, but he had a longtime girlfriend. But now after eight years they've finally broken up. I've joined his salsa class and tango class so I can get close to him again and it seems to be working. How long should I wait until I tell him how I feel? I don't want to rush him, but I also don't want some other girl to get in line ahead of me. Signed, Waiting for Mr. Wonderful' "

Rita sat straight up, as if someone had just connected her to an IV of espresso. "Matt Peruzzi," she murmured.

"Huh? No, it's this guy called 'The Dude.' He writes an advice column—didn't anyone tell him only chicks do that?"

"Mmmm-hmmmm," Rita murmured absentmindedly. Her heart was soaring. Could it be? she wondered. Could Gina have written to The Dude asking for advice? Had Rita's scheme to get Gina to take up tango and salsa with Matt actually worked?

Calvino was reading The Dude's response out loud. " 'Dear Waiting, Not to be harsh, but do you have any proof your love is requited? My guess is that if he could do without you for eight years, he can do without you a lot longer. What's I'm trying to say is: he's just not that into you. Do yourself a favor: find a guy in your salsa class who really wants to try out some five-pepper moves with you and go out with him instead. If Mr. Wonderful gets jealous, he'll make a move. If not, you've got your answer—and a guy who's probably a lot better for you than Mr. Wonderful. Because, remember, the real Mr. Wonderful is the guy who thinks you're wonderful, too.' "

Rita frowned. Now it was her turn to hope her ears were deceiving her. "That's terrible advice," she fumed. "Clearly, G—I mean, 'Waiting for Mr. Wonderful' — should wait for Mr. Wonderful. I mean, what's a few weeks or months after eight years?"

"Yeah. I mean," Calvino said, "who *is* this guy? Do you know The Dude?"

"Mmmm, yes," Rita said vaguely.

"I mean, he must be gay," Calvino said. "All that sensitive crap. 'The real Mr. Wonderful is the guy who thinks you're wonderful, too.' I mean—come on!"

"Calvino." Rita stood up. "You might try learning something from The Dude. After all, isn't that what Concetta wants? A little more sensitivity?"

She went to the refrigerator and tossed some leftover short ribs in the dog bowls, which sent Luciano and Cesare racing right over. Rita gave them each an affectionate pat on the head.

"He's not really that much more evolved," she said, winking at Calvino. "The Dude, that is. But he keeps trying, and that's what's important."

She slipped on her coat and grabbed her purse and keys.

"Where are you going?"

Calvino looked strangely panicked, the way her kids used to when she left them with Sal for the evening.

"To investigate."

"But what am I supposed to do?"

Rita thought a moment, then had a sudden flash of inspiration. She dashed into the family room, snatched a DVD case, and plunked it on the kitchen table. "I want you to watch all five hours of *Pride and Prejudice*," she said, "and then tell me how you think this relates to your recent tiff with Concetta. That's just a suggestion, of course, because I would not intervene in your love life for all the world. And here's another suggestion—the whole house could use vacuuming, the breakfast dishes need to be washed, and the bathrooms could use a good scrub."

"Say what?"

"The vacuum and the cleaning supplies are in the hall closet."

"But, I've never—"

"What? Cleaned in your life? Well, consider this an opportunity to learn. To grow as a husband. See you at six, if not before," she said as she sailed out the door. "*Ciao!*"

Chapter Fifteen

"Dead?" Julia Simms repeated for the third time.

Julia had apparently not read the *Morris County Gazette* yet that morning. In her current state, she reminded Rita of a robot whose circuits had overloaded; something did not compute.

Then Julia finally said something different, something that made Rita sit up straight on Julia's rose-colored loveseat: "Dead? Peggy? Why I just saw her—I can't believe it!"

"Peggy?" Rita said. "Who's Peggy? We're talking about Greta."

"Greta, Peggy, Margaret." Julia shrugged. "She kept changing her name, but I always thought of her as Peggy, because that was her name when we were growing up."

Rita smiled encouragingly. She had come merely to probe the butterfly tattoo connection, but she had stumbled onto a gold mine of information. Rita had thought that Greta and Julia had only become friends since Greta's arrival in Morris County, but clearly their association went much further back.

Which meant that Julia probably knew far more about the victim that Orlando did.

"Oh?" Rita reached for a shortbread cookie, took a sip of weak tea (while thanking her lucky stars that she was Italian), and settled back into the loveseat. "And where was that?"

"Binghampton."

Rita's mouth fell open and she nearly dropped her cookie into her teacup. Slightly down-at-the-heels, decidedly unglamorous Binghampton was the last place she could imagine the likes of Greta Giroux.

Of course, she reminded herself, she wasn't Greta back then.

"So how did you meet Greta, er, Peggy?"

"We moved to Binghampton when I was in second grade. On the first day of school, I made the mistake of saying that my dad was transferred there to be the plant manager. For the next week, kids would keep putting plants on my desk, in my bookbag, on my seat. And not nice plants, either—just mashed up dandelions or plants with thistles and thorns pulled out of some abandoned lot. And the minute I sat down on it or pulled it out of my book, someone would whisper 'plant lady' or 'feed me, Seymour' and everyone would start snickering."

"Children can be so cruel."

"Yes, but now, looking back on it, I realize it wasn't just cruelty, but also resentment. My dad was their dads' boss—at least, if their dad was still around and had a job. And I wore nice clothes and lived in a nice house, and we were some of the only people I knew who ever took a vacation that involved leaving the state."

"So—Peggy was one of the cruel kids?"

"Oh, no, not at all! She was nice as could be. After a week, she showed up at school with an actual potted plant—two of them, actually. She put one on her desk and one on mine and then started to decorate it with all these sparkly little bangles from the Dollar Store. And somehow it looked cool, not tacky, or at least Peggy convinced everyone it was cool. She said her mom, who was a model in L.A., said it was trendy out in California. She called them wishing trees."

"So Peggy made kids leave you alone by making you 'cool'?"

Julia smiled. "It was kind of the carrot and the stick with her. You could either be one of the cool kids and have one of these wishing trees, or if you really didn't come around, she'd threaten to tell her policeman dad about some illegal activity that kid's family member was involved in. She kept this little book, you see—like a little black book, but it had a unicorn sparkle cover. And in it, she wrote down whatever kids said in an unguarded moment—things they shouldn't, you know? And then she'd just bide her time until she needed that information."

Oh, the irony. Greta had been a blackmailer of sorts, and then she had become the blackmailed. And now she was dead.

"But she used her powers, so to speak, for good?" Rita asked.

"Of course."

Rita helped herself to another cookie. "So her mother was a model, huh? That explains her good looks. But why was she out in L.A. and Peggy/Greta left in Binghampton?"

"Oh." Julia looked embarrassed. "I'm not sure that was all exactly true. See, Greta made it sound like she was living with her aunt and uncle because her mom was some fabulous model in L.A. and her dad was too busy working as a cop. But her aunt and uncle weren't really her aunt and uncle, I found out later. They were foster parents. And I never saw any real evidence her mom was a model—or that they were even in touch much. I mean, one time she showed me a postcard from her mom from Venice Beach, but that was it. And it didn't say anything about being a model. It was pretty generic, really, something like 'Having fun in the sun; hope school is going well' or something like that. And her dad—or at least someone with the same last name, Wisniewski, who looked a lot like her—got arrested for a rash of burglaries our senior year. The paper said he had a long rap sheet. When I asked her about it, she just said cryptically that he wasn't her 'real dad.'"

"So, she spun a lot of fantasies?"

Julia poured them both another cup of tea, brought it to her lips, and then sat it down thoughtfully on the saucer. "You know, I could never decide if she believed her own stories or not. Is it a lie if the person who says it thinks it's true—wills it to be true?" She shook her head. "Somehow, you always got the sense, even when you found out that what she said wasn't strictly true, that there was some kernel of truth in it."

"Like maybe her mom really was a model in California? If she looked anything like Peggy/Greta, that wouldn't be hard to believe."

"Exactly. Plus, she made you want to believe her. She had that magic with everyone—the kids in school, their parents, the teachers and, of course, later the boys."

"So when did she become Greta Giroux? When she married?"

"Yes, but before that, she was Margaret Monroe. It happened sometime in college, so I don't know that much about it, because she was at SUNY Binghampton and I was at the University of Rochester. But the next thing I knew she'd transferred to SUNY Stony Brook and changed her name to Margaret Monroe. She said Monroe was her mother's stage name, and that she changed it partly to honor her mother, partly because she had a stalker and didn't want him to find her."

Rita put down her teacup. "A stalker? I wonder if he could have found her after all these years...Although it seems like if he was going to track her down, he would have done it long before now. Plus she has yet another name, so she'd be even harder to track. Where'd she pick up Giroux?"

"Her first husband, Pierre. He was a French-Canadian guy she met on a girls' weekend in Montreal. He had the cutest French accent. They had a whirlwind romance, spent probably six weekends together, and then got married."

"That seems rather hasty."

"Well, that was Peggy—or Margaret—at the time."

"And then she switched to Greta?"

Julia smiled over her teacup at Rita. "She said it had more panache."

"How long did that marriage last?"

"Oh, maybe two or three years. Once the whirlwind romance wore off, I think they found that they just didn't have much in common."

"And after that?"

"A series of boyfriends, but no one that serious until Orlando."

Frowning, Rita asked, "Is Pierre still around? Might he hold a grudge?"

"I think he went back to Canada and, last I heard, remarried."

"Is there anyone else you could imagine wanting to kill her?"

"Oh, no! Not a one."

Not for the first time, Rita thought Julia woefully naïve. Bianca had actually said she wanted Greta dead, Viola had certainly looked murderous, and to this must be added a former stalker.

"Julia," Rita said gently. "When I visited you in the hospital, you said perhaps it was a case of mistaken identity, and I think you were right. Yesterday wasn't the first attempt on Greta's life. The ball was."

Julia gasped. "Someone thought I was Greta?"

Rita reached over, gently turned Julia's wrist, slid her watch up, and lightly tapped the blue butterfly. "All anyone could see was that you were tall and slim and blonde...and that you had a butterfly tattoo."

Julia's lip was trembling now. She put her cup on her saucer with a clatter.

"How," Rita asked, "did you and Greta end up with the exact same tattoo?"

"In high school, our friend Jenny Farfalle died in a car crash. Farfalle means—"

"Butterflies."

"Oh, right—you would know, since it's Italian. So Peggy—Greta, that is—suggested we all get tattoos in her honor."

"Who else got the tattoo?"

"Meghan Mansfield, Susie Balistreri, and Katie O'Hara."

Rita jotted down their names. "So you've had this matching tattoo for almost three decades. I'm surprised I never noticed it before."

"Well, normally, it's covered by my watch." She held up her bony little wrist and the delicate, braided gold watch that hung loosely upon it. "But a watch didn't really go with my Renaissance costume."

Rita finished her tea and settled back into the couch. It was going to be a long morning.

"Now," Rita said, "walk me through exactly what you said and did and what everyone around you said and did, no matter how unimportant it seems, the night of the Carnevale ball."

Chapter Sixteen

"I arrived around seven," Julia began, "with my friend Sandy, the band teacher. We went down the stairs to the buffet. I had some chicken parm, some spaghetti with clams, and of course your desserts. Your *sanguinaccio* is my favorite. So creamy, so chocolatey."

Julia clapped her hands, and a look of rapture crossed her face. For a moment, she seemed to forget just why they were discussing what she ate.

"Whose chicken parm? Whose spaghetti?"

"Hmmmm?" Julia looked confused as she emerged from her chocolate reverie.

"Well, there were at least a dozen chicken parms and four *spaghetti alle vongole*."

"Oh—I don't remember whose they were."

"Well, was the chicken parm soggy, soupy, tough, or crispy? What was the cheese to red sauce ratio? Was it real provolone? And were the clams fresh or canned?"

Rita had a whole taxonomy of chicken parms and *spaghetti alle vongole* in her head, and if Julia could just answer a few simple questions, she was sure she could identify the cook.

"I really don't know," Julia said with a sigh, while Rita tried to hide her disappointment and frustration. Really, Julia was useless sometimes. No wonder she was so skinny; unless it was Rita's desserts, she paid no attention to what went into her mouth.

"Go on, then. What happened next?"

"Sandy and I saw Greta and Orlando."

"How did you know it was them?"

"Because I knew what they were wearing. I'd gone over there to try on costumes with Greta earlier in the day. She'd chosen a burgundy gown and I'd chosen an emerald green one."

Rita suddenly sat up very straight. "So you wore one of the gowns in Orlando's collection to the ball."

Flushing, Julia said, "Yes, although actually, Greta initially planned to wear the emerald green one, but when she tried it on, it was a little snug in the bust but"— Julia looked down at her chest and sighed—"it fit me perfectly."

Julia took a sip of tea. "And Orlando was wearing that awful costume with the beaked mask. I think he said it was the costume of a plague doctor. I guess it's very authentic but"—she wrinkled her cute little button nose— "I thought it was terrifying—and not very practical. I couldn't really hear anything he said through the beak. The sound was so muffled, and it was so loud in there. Plus, he had to keep lifting it up to eat."

"Greta talked a little about the wedding," Julia continued, "but she seemed kind of sad. At one point, she pointed at a woman in teal—Bianca, I assume—and said 'She hates me, you know. Her mother's poisoning her mind against me, and she's refusing to come to the wedding.' I tried to tell her that Bianca would come around, but Greta just said 'we'll see' like she didn't really believe me. Then I danced with a man in one of those masks that looks a little like Anonymous—"

"A *bauta* mask."

"Oh, yes—that's what Orlando said. He was about my height and a good dancer, but didn't say anything. Then a man in a red cape, kind of short and very sweaty, who kept stepping on my toes. He talked quite a lot, mostly about the food—he did praise your *teste di turco* to the high heavens—but I didn't recognize his voice. Then I danced with three or four other men I didn't recognize, neither tall nor short, fat nor thin, and neither particularly good nor bad dancers. Then Father de La Pasqua—his Roman collar gave him away. Then Paul Higgins, the chemistry teacher. His scent gave him away. Then Greta danced with Father De La Pasqua, so Orlando and I danced one song. Then we went over to the side of the room. Orlando saw someone he knew and went to talk to him. Greta and I talked to Dr. Stevens and her husband. I somehow managed to get a glob of cream from your *teste di turco* in my hair, so Dr. Stevens gave me her compact, and I struggled to get it out. Then Orlando re-appeared with two glasses of red

wine and handed one to me and one to Greta. Then
Orlando saw someone he knew again, went over to talk
to him, and Greta, Dr. Stevens, and her husband, and I
kept talking. At one point, someone bumped into Greta,
and Greta spilled half her wine. Greta claimed it was
Orlando's ex-wife Marie, although I don't know how she
could be sure."

"Did she bump into you, too?"

"Oh, no."

"Did you keep your eyes on your drink the whole
time, or were you too distracted by Marie or whoever
bumped Greta?"

"I...don't know."

"So someone could have slipped something into
your drink then?"

Julia quailed slightly. "I suppose so."

Rita considered this for a moment, then leaned
forward. "Are you absolutely one hundred percent sure
that the man who handed you the red wine was
Orlando?"

"Yes, of course."

"How?"

"Well, he was wearing that mask."

"Did he speak?"

Julia shook her head.

"Did he lift up his mask to eat or drink?"

"No."

"So how do you know?"

"But the mask—"

Rita shook her hand grimly. "I distinctly remember that there were two men," she said, "wearing the *medico delle peste* costume that night."

Rita did her best thinking while cooking, so she raced home from Julia's house and threw herself in a pasta-making frenzy, serenaded by the harpsichord music, clattering tea cups, and clip-clopping horses' hooves emanating from the family room. Calvino had followed her advice—mild suggestion, that is—and was watching *Pride and Prejudice*.

She dumped two generous handfuls of semolina flour onto her butchers' block, hollowed out a well in the center, and cracked three eggs into the well.

She stared at the yolks. Eyes.

What else had others seen?

Had anyone seen Orlando's ex-wife Marie bump Greta –and had that even been Marie? And more importantly, had anyone seen someone slip something into Julia's drink during this diversion, if that's even what that was? And would anyone else have seen anything to indicate whether Orlando—or the other *medico delle peste*—had brought Greta and Julia the wine?

She added some warm water, whisked the eggs and water with a fork, and started slowly chipping away at the sides of her well. As she gradually incorporated the flour into the eggs, an idea slowly formed in her mind.

She reached for the phone. "Orlando," she said, "would you like to come over for some comfort food right now? I'm in the middle of making pasta—I'll make any kind you like. And there's some leftover tiramisu for dessert."

Chapter Seventeen

An hour later, Rita was rolling long, thin, golden sheets of dough through her pasta maker and turning them into ribbons of fettucine before tossing them in a pot of salted boiling water.

"Extra prosciutto, extra butter, extra cream," Orlando requested with an attempt at a laugh as he leaned over the stovetop and watched Rita making the sauce. "It's not like I need to worry about fitting in my wedding suit."

"Oh, Orlando." She patted him on the back and dumped in more cream. "I'm so sorry. I didn't know her well, but I liked her. I really hoped you'd be happy together."

She chopped more prosciutto and tossed it into the pan. "How's Bianca taking it?"

"Well, I guess—almost too well."

"And the rest of the staff?"

"They're upset, naturally."

"All of them?" She peered over her glasses at him.

"Well," he said begrudgingly, "I did catch Viola humming this morning, but it's a bright, sunny day. And her sister is coming for a visit."

Rita knew for a fact that Viola and her sister did not get along, and Viola's sister was only coming to town so they could fight over their mother's will, but she decided it was better to let Orlando think her sister's visit was the reason Viola was so chipper. She took the saucepan off the burner and thinned the sauce with a splash of pasta water. Then she drained the pasta, divided it onto two plates, and poured the creamy sauce on top. Handing Orlando a glass of white wine and a plate, she motioned for him to follow her to the table, which was laden with crusty Italian bread, extra virgin olive oil, and a gleaming antipasti tray filled with marinated artichokes, Sicilian olives, sundried tomatoes, and roasted red peppers.

"So tell me," Rita said as she tucked enthusiastically into the pasta, "exactly what you saw and who you talked to the night of the Carnevale ball."

"The ball? What does that have to do with anything?"

"Because there are two possibilities. Either someone wanted to kill both Julia and Greta—and possibly every other woman who got a butterfly tattoo when their childhood friend Jenny Farfalle died thirty years ago—or someone thought Julia was Greta."

Orlando took a gulp of wine. His hand shook as he put his glass down.

"We arrived," he said, "around seven-thirty. Almost immediately, we spotted Julia and Sandy. I knew it was Julia, you see, because she was wearing an emerald green dress from my collection. We talked a lot about our wedding plans and Julia's upcoming trip to the Bahamas, plus the latest brouhaha over the band uniforms."

Rita raised an eyebrow.

"They were made in China," he explained, "and apparently some student was claiming they were made with slave labor in a prison camp."

"Ah."

"Sandy was quite upset, you see, because they have no money for other uniforms and if they don't wear uniforms to the state finals, they'll be disqualified."

Rita did not consider this a great loss, seeing as how the band had never made it to the semi-finals, but she could see why Sandy was so upset.

"I ate some of Lidia Caravaggio's lasagna, Jenny LaMotta's chicken parm, and of course your *sanguinaccio*."

Rita smiled. Unlike Julia, Orlando actually paid attention to what he ate.

"Then I danced with Greta for maybe a whole hour." He sighed. "It was wonderful. If I'd known that we'd have less than two weeks left together..."

His voice trailed off, his eyes were moist with unshed tears. He cleared his throat, slightly embarrassed, and went on. "Then she danced with Fred Von Beek, and I danced with Marion."

Rita did not need to ask him how he knew it was Marion.

"Then I think we each danced with a few more different people. I can't say who, really—a heavyset woman in red with a feathered headdress who kept trying to lead, a short woman who kept saying 'sorry, sorry' every time she stepped on my feet, and a woman in gray"—he colored— "who told me she'd make a better wife for me than Greta would."

Her face burning, Rita stared down at her plate and pretended to have trouble twirling her pasta round her fork. Her sister had been wearing a gray dress. Her sister had long carried a torch for Orlando. But surely....

"Her voice," he was saying, "was sort of familiar. Kind of brash—"

Rita waved her hand dismissively. "It's not that important, I'm sure." Brightly, she asked, "And after that?"

"Another two or three dances with Greta, then a couple more with not very memorable women—honestly, I can't even remember what color they were wearing. And then Greta danced with Father De La Pasqua, and I danced with Julia. I was pretty tired after dancing for nearly two hours, so we went over to the side of the room, near a pillar, fairly close to the buffet table. Then I saw Tony Zappa, whose construction company put in a bid for the winery expansion—if, that is, it's ever approved." He sighed. "Not that I find myself caring a whole lot now. Without Greta, it all seems rather pointless. And it was her dream, anyway—not mine. So I went to talk to Tony, and then he introduced me to his wife, who introduced me to her sister, who owns a restaurant in Albany that might want to carry our wines. One thing led to another and the next thing I knew, Julia had collapsed and I ran over to see what I could do to help."

"So you never brought Greta and Julia two glasses of wine?"

He frowned and thought for a moment. "Early in the night, I think I did."

"But, say, within a half hour of Julia collapsing?"

"No—why?"

"Because she collapsed after drinking wine that she thought she got from you."

Chapter Eighteen

There were over one hundred guests at Greta's visitation, and Rita recognized all but a few of them.

"I didn't think to put it in the Binghampton paper," Julia murmured apologetically in Rita's ear. "I called Katie and Susie, but that was it. And they couldn't come on such short notice."

For a moment, Rita didn't recognize the names. Then she said, "Ah—the butterfly tattoo gang. And her foster parents?"

Julia sighed. "Either their number is unlisted—or they've passed away."

Calvino and Sal lumbered up to them. Sal had cleaned up pretty well in a black suit and tie, and for once he was clean shaven. He looked uncomfortable, the way he always did at funerals, as if he suddenly remembered his days were numbered.

Calvino had tried to pour himself, rather unsuccessfully, into one of Sal's old suits. His neck bulged over the collar of a borrowed white dress shirt. The first few buttons were undone, and a carpet of salt-and-pepper chest hair peeked out. It was the stuff of nightmares, Rita thought—like a creeping vine that had a mind all its own and could never be tamed.

Calvino took a swig from his coffee cup, wiped his mouth with the back of his hand, and shook his head. "Reminds me of the wake for Uncle Louie," he said, punching Sal on the arm. "Remember that? A couple of goombas showed up just to make sure he was really dead. One just reached right in there and stuck a big needle in him, I guess thinking that would make him sit up."

"Calvino!" Rita hissed while propping Julia up beside her. Julia looked as though she were about to faint.

"Yeah," Calvino said, completely unfazed, "it was kinda awful. Zia Anita got out a baseball bat and chased them away with some real colorful cusswords. I think she called him a—"

"Calvino!" Rita's voice has ratcheted up several octaves, and this time a dozen people turned to stare at them.

When the onlookers had turned back around, Calvino tried to mollify Rita. "But this is totally different, see? They were Uncle Louie's bookies and just wanted to make sure he wasn't trying to weasel out of his debts. And he mighta been diddling one of their wives—"

"Bianca! Gina!" Rita suddenly cried out, latching onto her daughter and her friend as they passed by and yanking them towards her in an attempt to interrupt Calvino's completely inappropriate walk down memory lane.

Everyone gave each other the customary two *bacci* on the cheek, except for Julia, who despite living in a heavily

Italian-American community for a couple of decades, always seemed confused—or perhaps even slightly repulsed—by all of the kissing.

"How are you holding up, *cara?*" Rita said to Bianca, casting a critical eye over Bianca's solemn face. Her eyes were bright and clear, however, neither red-rimmed nor puffy. She did not appear to have shed a tear over Greta.

"I'm—well—" Bianca turned for a moment and shot a guilty glance at the casket. She finally settled on saying, "I'd be lying if I said we were the best of friends, or that I wanted her to be my stepmother. But I just wanted them to break up...not this. I mean, I know what I said"—she flushed—"but I didn't really mean it. Not literally."

Rita patted Bianca's back, remembering the time Bianca had been inconsolable when their pet rabbit had died. She had blamed herself for forgetting to put fresh carrots in their cardboard box in the morning, but Rita had convinced her that the orphaned baby bunny had instead died of a broken heart.

"I feel terrible for my dad," Bianca said. "It's awful to see him suffer this way."

At this, Bianca's dark eyes did actually fill with tears.

"Come on," Gina said, pulling Bianca along. "Let's get you some coffee."

"I'll come with you," Julia said, and they drifted off together.

Rita turned to Calvino, her fury building. "How could you," she fumed, "bring up Sal's black sheep relatives at a funeral of all places and make everyone's stomachs turn with tales of mobsters poking pins into corpses?"

"It was a needle," he said with infuriating equanimity, "and it was totally just like this wake. First, I was in line to, uh, pay my respects to Greta—and I gotta tell you, that mortician did a bang-up job making a dead chick look hot—behind that mousy chick from the hike in the woods."

"McKenzie?"

"Yeah, that's the one. The one that makes my favorite cheesecake at the Sunshine Café. Yeah, so she's with her boyfriend and she says to him, 'Someone should stick a stake in her heart, just to make sure.'"

Rita frowned.

"Like she was a zombie," Calvino said, "you know? Or a vampire."

"How did Luca react?"

"Just shushed her up. Then this lady with all this bling on her fingers—"

"Aria?"

"No, it was an older lady."

"It was Marie," Sal interjected. "The ex-wife."

A look of sudden understanding suffused Calvino's face. "Yeah, so the ex goes up to the casket, laughs, and says 'guess you're not taking over, toots.'"

Rita remembered how Julia had said Marie had bumped into Greta at the ball. Maybe that hadn't been an accident. And maybe Marie still had designs on Orlando—or at least on the winery they had built together.

"I'm surprised she even came," Rita said, "but maybe she came to give Bianca—or even Orlando—emotional support."

She turned to observe Orlando, who was grasping the hand of one gray-haired little bird of a woman. Probably an elderly aunt, Rita surmised.

Orlando was doubled over as if in pain, his face long and drawn and his eyes red and puffy. He had aged ten years overnight. Viola, perhaps predictably, was at his side, bringing mourners to him and then dispatching them with her customary efficiency.

"Poor Orlando," she murmured. "*Poverino.*"

"Yeah," Calvino said, " 'cuz Greta was kinda a hottie."

Rita slugged him on the arm, hard.

"And they were probably soulmates," Calvino added quickly. "Like Elizabeth and Darcy." The corners of his mouth dropped down. "Or me and Concetta. I wish I could go off on my white horse and save the day and prove my love like Darcy, but Concetta doesn't have a slutty little sister in need of saving."

"Calvino—"

"Okay, she does have kinda a slutty sister, but she's fifty-seven and lives in a double wide in South Florida and there's not much I can do. The point is, Rita, I love Concetta and we're gonna kick the bucket sooner rather than later. And I don't wanna waste the time we have left. So can you talk to Concetta? *Per piacere?*"

Rita's eyes pricked with tears. It was probably the most eloquent Calvino had ever been. It was a low bar, but still....

"Calvino—" she began, but she was immediately interrupted by Father De La Pasqua.

"What a sad day," he said, giving Sal and Calvino each a manly thump on the back and then leaning in to give Rita two *bacci* on the cheek. "And to think I danced with Greta at the ball. She was so full of life, so excited about the wedding." He sighed, then seemed to remember he was a priest. "Well, she's with our Heavenly Father now. I guess we have to console ourselves with that."

Father De La Pasqua took a sip of red wine. "How's your Lenten resolution going, Rita?" He pointed at Sal and Calvino. "I hope you two are keeping her honest. No meddling, er, interfering, whatsoever."

Sal grunted noncommittally, and Calvino said, "I liked it better when Rita gave up chocolate."

Father De La Pasqua just nodded affably and pushed his way through the crowd to greet the next parishioner.

"You heard what he said," Rita pouted. "I can't call Concetta. You have to patch things up yourself."

"Well, how can I do that if she won't even pick up the phone? And I mean, what does he know? He's never been married."

"He's a *priest.*"

"I rest my case."

Out of the corner of her eye, she caught a glimpse of Matt Peruzzi in one corner of the funeral parlor, her daughter Gina in another. Rita excused herself and then made a beeline for her daughter.

Gina was talking to Jack MacDougall, who seemed to be midway through telling her how Orlando and Greta had met. "She was having car trouble, so she pulled off onto the shoulder on the way up Passamaquody Mountain and Orlando came over and looked under the hood and—oh, hello, Mrs. Calabrese."

"Hello, Jack. What a sad day. How is the staff holding up?"

"It's tough, you know? She was still sort of young and definitely full of life. She had lots of new ideas, too, like the winery expansion."

Her gaze followed his as he turned to look at Teri, Diana, and Aria, who were huddled together, immaculately turned out, their glossy newscaster tresses falling halfway down their backs. They had had the audacity to fasten their pins protesting the winery expansion to their little black dresses, which Rita found to be far sexier than the occasion required.

"Viola's been great," Jack said, nodding in her direction. "She's been a rock for Orlando. But then, she's always been there for Orlando—at least, that's what everyone says."

"Mmmm," Rita murmured rather ambiguously. "That's Viola for you—quite incredible." She saw that Matt and his mother were getting their coats on. If she dilly-dallied another moment, they'd be gone and she'd have missed her chance to get her daughter and her future son-in-law together. She decided it didn't count as meddling if she simply took Gina with her to talk to Mrs. Peruzzi. "Now," she said to Jack, "if I could just borrow Gina for a moment—"

"Of course." To Gina, he added, "Shoot me a text when you want to meet up and go birding."

"Birding!" Rita hissed as she slipped one arm through Gina's and pulled her along. "You couldn't tell a Vermilion flycatcher from a vulture. Since when have you been into birds?"

"Since now."

Gina had a strange dreamy look in her eyes. Rita hoped it was because she had already spotted Matt across the room.

"Jack is very knowledgeable about birds," Gina said. "He was an Outward Bound counselor and wants to get into teaching. But he needs to get his teaching certificate so he's working at the winery—"

Rita made a frantic gesture to Marion, who was lurking by the door, so that Marion would keep the Peruzzis from leaving.

"Oh!" Marion shouted. Her voice carried across the entire funeral parlor. Everyone looked up from their coffee and cheese plates.

"Agnes, I haven't seen you in ages," Marion shrieked, "and you're just the person I need to talk to."

Marion went into excruciating detail about her cousin's latest medical diagnosis and begged Agnes for advice, since apparently Agnes suffered from the same malady. Agnes was a bit of a hypochondriac and never missed a chance to discuss her health, so this was a brilliant strategy.

Rita and Gina finally reached their little circle. "Oh, Marion," Rita said, "I have the most wonderful news! Sue Ferrara is interested in joining the quilting circle, but I didn't have all the details, so you must go and speak to her. And Agnes, Sal's gout has flared up again, and I really need you to talk to him. You know how fond he is of sweets, but I told him the anti-inflammatory diet you were on did wonders for your health...."

She led both women away, trying to hide the smile that spread across her face. She turned back only once, just in time to see Gina cross her arms and say, "So, I hear you broke up with Morgan."

Chapter Nineteen

A half an hour later, as Rita helped herself to a glass of red wine and another cheese plate—Rita felt that drowning one's sorrows in dairy was a suitable grieving mechanism—Gina came up behind her and hissed in her ear, "If that wasn't meddling, what was it?"

"Your father needed medical advice," Rita said innocently. "And I wanted to talk to an old friend and neighbor. I can't help it if she's Matt's mother. Besides, how did I meddle? I didn't say a single word to Matt."

Out of the corner of her eye, Rita saw McKenzie put on her coat and head out the door, Luca on her arm. More to herself than to Gina, Rita said softly, "I wish I knew why she hated Greta."

"Oh, that's easy." Gina helped herself to another glass of wine and took a sip. "A year and a half ago, before Greta met Orlando, when she was new in town, she worked at the library."

Rita's ears perked up. McKenzie's mother had been the head librarian for the past thirty years.

"Greta had all of these ideas," Gina said, "about 'modernizing' the library and making it 'Morris County's living room,' a 'hub of innovation and creativity.' She thought they needed a capital campaign to add on this crazy glass atrium and have a 'maker space' and she wanted to host author talks and robotics competitions. She even wanted to sell half of the collection to free up room so they could create more meeting rooms and space for 'community gatherings.' She said Michelle"—Michelle was McKenzie's mother—"was standing in the way of progress and maybe it was time for her to retire."

"Well," Rita huffed, feeling affronted on behalf of Michelle and every sixty-something woman who'd ever been assailed by some perky, self-righteous, clueless Gen Xer, "I can see why Michelle would be upset. She *built* that collection."

"Yeah. Lucky for Michelle, then Greta met Orlando and decided to re-make the winery instead of the library. Plus, being Orlando's wife paid a little more"—Gina rubbed her fingers together—"than being head librarian."

Gina took a bite of cheese and closed her eyes in ecstasy. "Wow, this is good. The woman did know her cheese, at least. Oh—and here's another reason McKenzie hated Greta. Greta claimed there was a bug in her soup at the Sunshine Café during McKenzie's shift and called the health department."

Rita chuckled. "Good thing the head of the health department is a regular."

"Yeah, but McKenzie almost lost her job, and she never forgave her." Gina frowned. "Hey, can you do me a favor? Can you check up on Jack?"

"Jack? Whatever for?"

"Well, he's exactly the opposite of the kind of guy I normally go for, and the definition of stupidity is doing the same thing over and over again and expecting different results, so I thought..."

Rita looked over at Jack, who was being ordered around by Viola, and sighed. "Can't you just Google him?"

Gina shook her head. "I tried. I can't find much. He won a swim meet in high school, and that's about it."

"*Mi dispiace,*" Rita said, kissing her daughter on the cheek. "But a certain child of mine begged me to take a vow not to intervene, remember? So I cannot—could not, would not—intervene."

"Could not, would not? What are you—Dr. Seuss?"

"You're on your own this time, *cara*. And if I were going to intervene, trust me—all my efforts would be to support a match with Matt Peruzzi. Jack's sweet, I suppose, but he's a little young for you and he seems rather immature, a little simple even. He's no match for my brilliant daughter—you'd run circles around him. But Matt Peruzzi—now that's what I call a catch."

When her editor called the next morning, Rita had just finished breakfast and was whipping up a batch of *sanguinaccio*—minus the pigs' blood, which was hard to come by. Until now, she'd taken far too little advantage of *not* having given up chocolate for Lent, and she resolved to change that.

"Hello, Sam!" she shouted as she briskly whisked together frothing hot milk, dark velvety cocoa powder, sugar, and flour.

"I hope that's the sound of the wheels in your brain turning," Sam grunted, "because I need another story. Several, in fact. Half the newsroom has come down with the flu. I need something for the arts section, and of course something sensational for the front page. Good job on the funeral story, by the way. It really tugged at the heartstrings."

Rita was so surprised she almost failed to notice that the cocoa mixture was now thick and boiling and needed to be removed from the heat. She had never thought Sam had any heartstrings to pull, particularly for someone like Greta Giroux.

"Any new developments?" Sam said gruffly. "On the case, that is? Did anyone call you after yesterday's deadline and beg to confess? Anyone try to run Orlando off the road on his way home?"

Rita sighed. Really, sometimes Sam had the most vivid imagination.

"No." Rita glared at the phone, as if to communicate her displeasure at Sam's lack of sensitivity through the phone line. "As far as I know, everyone made it home safely. *Per fortuna.*"

Rita tossed in dark brown, almost black, shards of Valhrona 72 percent dark chocolate. Valhrona was the world's silkiest, smoothest, most luxurious chocolate, and it was imported from the tiny town of Tain-L'Hermitage in southern France. Rita was loath to admit that anything French could be superior to anything Italian, but in this particular case, it would be a crime not to.

As the Valhrona melted slowly into the bubbling, chocolatey mixture and Rita kept whisking, Rita looked around the room frantically, searching for inspiration. Luciano and Cesare were strategically lying by the refrigerator, waiting for someone to open the doors and drop some tasty morsel. Sal and Calvino were lounging at the kitchen table in ratty wifebeaters and bathrobes, their bare feet propped up on the table as always, no matter how many times she asked them not to. They were both reading the *Morris County Gazette*, although she noticed that they'd given her story on the funeral a pass. Instead, Sal was devouring the sports page, and Calvino was loudly heaping opprobrium on The Dude's latest column.

"Well," Rita said lamely, cradling the phone between her neck and her shoulder, "Julia Simms talked with Larry Stevens at the Carnevale ball, and apparently he's writing a play that's a version of *The Legend of Sleepy Hollow*, but with aliens."

"Aliens!"

The clicks on the line grew louder and faster. Rita could tell Sam was flicking her tongue ring against her teeth, the way she always did when irritated.

"Who would want to see that?" Sam fumed. "Here's a headline for you: 'Morris County: Where Art and Culture Come to Die.' Maybe we should just replace the Arts section with the train schedule to New York, since that's apparently the only way to get culture. Aliens! I mean, why not Shakespeare with robots or *My Fair Lady* set in a Thai brothel?"

Well, Rita thought, maybe those were Larry's next projects. She tossed a dash of homemade vanilla extract, distilled from the world's best pure Hawaiian vanilla beans, into the mixture, which now was a thick sludge, and moved the phone away from her ear. From past experience, she knew that Sam was liable to go on and on, since the supposed backwardness of Morris County was one of Sam's favorite topics. Rita rather thought that Sam doth protest too much. After all, Sam never actually made any plans to move back to Buffalo—which Sam romanticized as a hotbed of crime and corruption (conveniently forgetting that parts of it were lovely and even trendy right now), a veritable cornucopia of material for dogged journalists—nor did she make plans to move anywhere else.

"Plus, no one reads anymore," Sam was griping. "It's all about the photos. What would we even photograph? It's not been produced yet. Of course, maybe we could just re-run the photos Old Van Dusen sent us right before he died of the UFO he claimed to have spotted...."

Rita mixed the vanilla in thoroughly, poured the mixture into individual ramekins, and set them on a tray to cool.

Across the room, Calvino belched loudly and said, "Get a load of this. 'Dear Dude, a guy who apparently has a lot of mojo (although he doesn't seem that special to me) started taking tango classes, and now every single woman in the county is signed up. So I signed up, too, because he can't go out with all of them, right? I met a woman who's thirteen years older than me in the class, and I'm really into her. The problem is she's still into the guy with the mojo, even though he's not into her. Honestly, that tango class is like having *The Bachelor* right here in Morris County.' "

Meanwhile, on the phone, Sam had really warmed to her subject by now, spinning her own dark theories about what Old Van Dusen really saw. With a gleam in her eye, Rita waited until Sam took a breath and then interrupted with, "Forget the aliens, Sam. How about a special on the tango craze sweeping Morris County? We could get some great action shots and lots of quotes. Maybe a love story or two."

"I like it!" Sam said. "Then everyone quoted will buy a paper. Maybe we can even get an ad buy out of it—you know, advertising tango classes, tango outfits, etcetera."

Totally oblivious to the fact Rita was trying to talk on the phone, Calvino continued reading in a loud voice.

"'So what should I do? Should I tell her how I feel? Or is it pointless while she's making googly eyes at The Bachelor? And will she think I'm too young? Signed, One Confused Dude in Love with a Cougar.'"

"Now," Sam was saying, "for the front page, you've got to get me something more on Greta's murder—or a new murder. Take your pick. If it bleeds—"

Rita chimed in, and they finished the sentence in unison. "—it leads."

But then Rita frowned. The truth was that the salacious details she had uncovered hadn't yet been made public: the fact that Julia and Greta had matching tattoos, and that Julia's poisoning was most likely an attempt on Greta's life; the fact that Julia had accepted wine from someone in a *medico delle peste* costume, and Orlando had claimed it wasn't he.

But she had a sneaking suspicion that releasing these details would just spook the murderer—and make it even harder to solve the case.

Stalling for time, Rita said, "Well, all murders are ultimately about the relationship between the murderer and the victim. Now, we don't know the killer—yet—but we know who the victim is. At least, we know her name. But we don't really know much about her past. She was only in town about a year and half before she was killed."

"Mmmm." Sam sounded intrigued. "Maybe she had some skeletons in her closet. Maybe she was actually a man and someone found out. Or maybe she was in witness protection; maybe she was a former moll for the mob."

Rita tried not to laugh.

"Hah!" Calvino shouted, his meaty palm coming down with a smack on the newsprint. "Listen to what this *cretino*, The Dude, has to say! 'Dear One Confused Dude, for one thing, stop calling her a 'cougar'; women hate that. I'm guessing The Bachelor is better looking than you, has a better job, and is probably more charming—that's why every woman is after him and not you. But you're right—the numbers are in your favor. My advice? Bide your time, be 'the friend,' and be the shoulder to cry on when he bonks someone else. You can't compete in most ways, but you can be Mr. Sensitive. Plus, when she feels rejected, having a younger man into her will be a big ego boost. Good luck! The Dude.'"

Calvino threw down the paper in disgust. "Darcy wasn't charming or sensitive at all, and he got the girl. I mean, who *is* this guy? Why does anyone bother reading him?" He shook his head and poked his cousin in the arm. "I mean, can you believe The Dude?"

Sal flushed and shrugged. "I read him sometimes. It's kinda interesting just to see what he says."

Rita covered her phone and said to Calvino, "It's one of the *Morris County Gazette*'s most popular features. And, as a woman, I can tell you that it's often sound advice—except, of course, for that advice to the young woman in the tango class last week. That was terrible."

Sal shook his head and mumbled, "I thought it was pretty good."

Still listening to Sam's wild ideas about all the skeletons that could be in Greta's closet, Rita opened the fridge, tossed some leftover *bistecca alla fiorentina* in Luciano and Cesare's bowls, provoking wild canine ecstasy, and walked over to the kitchen table.

"Don't worry, Sam. Sal"—she picked up his bare hairy feet and let them fall to the floor—"will accompany me to the tango class tonight. I'll get you a great story by noon tomorrow."

Sal's eyes bugged out, and he muttered something under his breath.

"And Calvino" –Rita picked up Calvino's feet, even hairier and dirtier than Sal's, and plopped them on the floor—"will then accompany me on a lovely road trip to Binghampton, where he will help me uncover those skeletons in Peggy Wisniewski-slash-Margaret-Monroe-slash-Greta-Giroux's closet."

Chapter Twenty

"One Confused Dude in Love with a Cougar" had not exaggerated. Enrollment in the tango class at the Mount Washington Community Center had swelled from thirty to over two hundred, with bodies packed so tightly that the big, bold steps of the fiery dance had to be reduced to tiny mincing steps to keep everyone from careening into each other.

Rita and Sal did not have to guess at the cause.

"Well, there's The Bachelor himself," Sal grunted in Rita's ear as they spotted the knot of women around Matt Peruzzi. "But it's a little hard to say who the cougar is."

Rita hung her head. "Is there any hope for our Gina? Look at the competition."

"Are you kidding? Who wouldn't want to date Gina? She's the smartest, best-looking gal here." Sal had that adorable gruffly affectionate tone in his voice. He winked. "*Certo*, except for you, *cara*."

The tango instructor, a leggy woman with platinum blonde hair and jet-black roots, clapped her hands and, in an alluring Argentine accent, ordered them to take their places.

Rita and Sal wedged themselves between two couples: Matt Peruzzi and Bianca Rinaldi, and Vinnie and McKenzie.

Well, Rita thought, this evening just got more interesting.

"*Figlio*," she said, addressing Vinnie, "I didn't expect to see you here."

Vinnie had always refused to dance at family weddings, maintaining that he was "allergic" to dancing.

Vinnie flushed. Clearly, he was just as surprised to see his parents. "Oh, uh...just expanding my horizons, Ma, the way you always tell me to."

"Good for you, Vin. And McKenzie—I didn't know you danced. Where's Luca?"

"Working." She sighed. "The restaurant business is a lot of nights and weekends. I finally decided that if I wanted to tango, I'd have to take lessons without him."

Rita noticed that McKenzie seemed to be the one woman in the room not looking longingly at Matt Peruzzi, so perhaps this was the truth.

"*Buona sera*, Bianca," Rita said, turning to her left. She nodded curtly at Bianca's partner. She realized it was silly, but she felt rather affronted that Matt was dancing with Bianca instead of her lovely, lovelorn daughter, who was stuck with Paul Higgins, the chemistry teacher, who no doubt reeked of his latest experiment.

The instructor and her partner demonstrated the basic walking step and the walking turn once again.

Then the music began. It was a mournful tune, all wailing violins and accordions, and the singer had the deep throaty voice of a woman who'd chain-smoked her way through a lifetime of hard living.

"Now everyone in closed position!" the instructor announced. "Remember, bend at the knees and men, press lightly so the woman feels the lead. Here we go—slow, slow, quick, quick, slow."

"You don't think our Vinnie is 'Confused,' do you?" Rita murmured as she and Sal took three steps back, then dragged their feet to the side.

Sal chuckled in her ear, and his stubble brushed her cheek. "Are you kidding? Vinnie—in love with an older woman? He'd be more likely to write in about a high school girl—someone more on his level."

Rita floated along, guided by Sal's strong lead. Despite his earlier bellyaching, he seemed to be enjoying himself. Sal always had been surprisingly light on his feet.

Then the song ended, and the instructor asked them to change partners.

"Remember," Rita said to Sal as she gave him a squeeze, "to ask McKenzie about Greta."

"Isn't that meddling?"

"It doesn't count," Rita said, "if it's in the service of the greater good, and solving a murder is definitely for the greater good."

"Ah." Sal sounded amused.

Rita accepted Matt's graciously extended hand. It was soft and warm and all rather thrilling. She could see why he got all the single ladies' hearts racing. Now if only Gina could snag him before some other woman snapped him up....

She craned her neck to look at her daughter and saw that Gina was now suffering through the attentions of Jack MacDougall, who was demonstrating bird calls with a fist held up to his lips while they waited for the music to begin. Rita sighed. Her daughter really did have rotten luck.

"Matt," she said brightly, "it was so nice seeing you and your mother at the funeral. Agnes gave Sal such wonderful advice about his gout. Why, look at him now—dancing!"

"Glad to hear it, Mrs. C. You guys are like family to me."

Rita's heart fluttered. We could actually be family, she thought, if only you'd send these other girls packing and focus on Gina.

"I think of you like a son, too," Rita gushed. "That's why I was so upset to hear about your breakup with Morgan. She was a sweet girl."

Matt smiled ruefully. "Yeah, that was tough."

"But sometimes when one door closes, another opens. You know, when I was in high school, I knew Sal of course, and we dated a little, but my heart belonged to Stefano Finocchiaro. He was *bellissimo*. But that didn't work out and then years later I re-connected with Sal, and it just seemed like coming home. And we've been happily married for over forty years."

Matt executed a walking turn. "That's wonderful," he said. "Morgan and I didn't even make eight."

"But you weren't married, so that's different. But when you meet—or re-connect—with someone who's ready to commit, who shares your values, you will find a relationship that will last forty or fifty years." She glanced over at Gina and willed him to follow her gaze. Unfortunately, Gina seemed to be wrapped up in her conversation with Jack. "Maybe someone Italian, someone Catholic. Someone who's really settled, you know? With a house and a good job. Morgan always seemed a little at loose ends to me, maybe just not ready to settle down."

He sighed. "Well, with me, anyway."

The music ended abruptly.

"And change partners!" the instructor shouted. "And remember, we have extra women, so some women need to dance together."

Rita was about to rotate again and dance with a sandy-haired, freckle-faced boy—one of the O'Day boys, she thought—when Gina bore down on her and snatched her up.

"Women need to dance with women," Gina tsk-tsked as she led Rita away. "I'll lead."

The music started again, and Gina's palms pressed into Rita's, driving her backwards in large, dramatic steps. "Mother," she hissed, "you are making a spectacle of yourself."

"*Moi?*" Rita said innocently. "I'm here in my capacity as a journalist. I'm writing an article about the soaring popularity of tango in Morris County. Would you like to give a quote?"

"No." Gina turned Rita abruptly. "And what were you saying to Matt Peruzzi just now?"

"Just the usual. 'How are you? How's your family?' That sort of thing."

"Mmmm-hmmm." Gina did not sound convinced.

"How's Jack? Did you ever go bird-watching?"

"As a matter of fact, we did—and it was lovely, no thanks to you."

"Me?"

"Well, if he'd been an axe murderer, he could have killed me."

"But he didn't."

"Right. But I had to go bird-watching with him without knowing that he wasn't going to kill me. Because my mother—who never passes a chance to check up on anyone—refused to check up on him."

"Well, *cara*, you didn't want me to meddle...so I didn't."

"It's not meddling if someone asks." Gina's strides became even longer, and Rita struggled to follow. "And speaking of things you should intervene in—but probably won't—Rocco and Vinnie are going on Spring Break to South Carolina. No good can come of that."

"He's an adult, *cara*." Rita craned her neck and watched Vinnie lead his partner, a very horrified-looking Bianca, crashing into a middle-aged couple. This caused a chain reaction, and pretty soon Vinnie's corner of the room more closely resembled a bumper car pavilion than a dancehall. Rita winced. "Technically. Speaking of which, how old is Jack? Isn't he a bit young for you?"

Gina shrugged. "Mid-twenties. Older than Vinnie."

"Yes, but you're thirty-four, *figlia*."

"So? No one would say anything if the ages were reversed. Look at Orlando and Greta. He is sixty-ish, and she was what—forty?"

"Forty-seven, actually. She looked younger than she was."

The music ended. Out of the corner of her eye, she saw Bianca making a beeline for Matt Peruzzi. Rita caught Sal's eye, and he stopped Bianca, reaching out his hand to dance. Rita hustled over with Gina.

"Actually," she said, "why don't you dance with your daughter? Bianca and I can catch up, plus it really would be good for me to practice leading."

She led a disappointed Bianca to the corner of the room, noting with satisfaction that Matt was dancing with old Mrs. Fauci. Sal and Gina were smack-dab next to them, all the better to facilitate a partner exchange for the next dance.

"Are you having a good time?" Rita asked pleasantly. "My, you're light on your feet!"

"I enjoy it," Bianca said. "It really takes away the stresses of the workday, and it's a good way to meet people."

Rita noticed that Bianca's gaze was fixed on Matt as she said this, so Rita abruptly turned Bianca towards the wall.

"Can I get a quote from you later for the paper?"

"Sure. I'll text it to you later."

"And have you met anyone in particular?"

"Oh—no." Bianca turned pink. "Not yet, anyway."

Rita tried to lead Bianca in a turn, but she misjudged the turning radius and they almost bumped into Marge from bridge club and her husband.

"Oh, dear," Rita sighed. "Perhaps you should lead, Bianca. There—that's better. You know, there's one thing I've been wondering. Why did you go out onto the ice during the foraging expedition?"

Bianca colored, but this time out of a different kind of embarrassment. "Someone slipped me a note, asking me to meet at that big bush right by the shoreline—and, unluckily for me, the incline by that bush was quite slippery. They said they had information on Greta. So I thought—I thought..."

Her voice trailed off and she tripped over Rita's feet. Catching herself, she mumbled an apology and then said, "It doesn't matter now. It was silly anyway, thinking I could stop the wedding, thinking that I *should* stop the wedding. I was so sure she was a gold-digger and didn't really love my dad." She shrugged. "Maybe she was and maybe she wasn't. I guess now we'll never know. But what I do know now is that she made my dad happy, and that's more important than money. He's miserable these days, just moping around the winery. The only people he talks to are me and Viola."

"Viola," Rita murmured. "She and your dad are close, aren't they?"

Wrinkling her nose, Gina said, "Well, not in that way. It's all business."

"For both of them?"

"Well, for him anyway."

Interesting, Rita thought. So Bianca also suspected Viola carried a torch for her dad.

"Who was the note from?"

"I don't know. It was hand-written—sort of messy. All block letters, blue pen. But I didn't recognize the writing."

"And where's the note now?"

"At the bottom of the pond," Bianca said ruefully, "along with my beautiful suede boots. Why? Does it matter?"

Rita squeezed her hand. "Probably not. *Non ti preocupare, cara.*"

Their dance ended, and Rita thanked Bianca. Once Sal deftly handed Gina off to Matt Peruzzi, she breathed a sigh of relief. Then, she walked around, jotting down quotes and "meet-cute" stories and checking to make sure Rocco, the *Morris County Gazette* photographer, was getting all of the photos they needed.

"Did you get one of Matt and Gina?" she asked.

Rocco fidgeted and looked down at the floor. "Uh, no, I don't think so."

"Well, go get one then!" She shooed him across the dance floor. "They're very photogenic, very front-page material."

Rita started whistling under her breath, imagining Matt and Gina ten years from now, showing their three angelic, Mass-attending, Italian-speaking, *nonna*-adoring children a musty, yellowed front page of the *Morris County Gazette* and saying, "This is the moment we reconnected—caught on film."

She felt someone brush his lips over her cheek.

"Sal!" She spun around.

Her took her in his arms and led her across the room. "Mission accomplished," he said with a wink. "No smoking gun, *cara*, but that McKenzie, well, let's just say her mother apparently never told her"—he whistled and lowered his voice, switching to Italian in case he was overheard—"*non parlare male dei morti.*"

Sal might be right, Rita thought. McKenzie's mother might never have told her not to speak ill of the dead. But it was just as likely that McKenzie's mother had—but made an exception for the woman who'd tried to force her out as head librarian of the Morris County Library.

Chapter Twenty-One

Her editor was pleased with Rita's story, and the photo of Matt and Gina made the front page.

Gina was rather less pleased. "Nice photo," she grunted in one of their customarily terse phone conversations as Rita sprawled on her couch, savoring a *sanguinaccio* while Luciano and Cesare dozed beside her.

"Well, you were the most photogenic couple there. It's as simple as that."

"We're not a couple, Ma."

"So you keep saying."

To Rita's surprise, Gina let that one go. "Ma, I was wondering if you were going to quilting circle anytime soon. It's promotion time soon, you know...."

Gina trailed off to let her mother fill in the blanks—which Rita could, perfectly. Mrs. Glenn was in her quilting circle, and she was married to Gina's boss.

"*Cara,*" Rita said, shaking her head, "I'm gorging myself on *sanguinaccio* right now. Why? Because a certain daughter of mine told me not to meddle. Now, you can't have it both ways. Either I meddle or I don't. And right now, I won't. So, you're on your own."

She stabbed the "off" button and took a particularly big spoonful of *sanguinaccio*. Luciano opened one eye and raised one pointy ear.

"Gina," she said as if in answer to his silent question. "*Mamma mia*—there's no pleasing that girl."

With a grunt, Luciano lumbered up, turned tail, and plopped down again.

"My thoughts exactly," Rita snapped. "Plus, she interrupted my train of thought. I was just getting somewhere with cross-referencing the list of participants in the foraging expedition with a list of people known to have attended the St. Vincent's Carnevale ball. Of course, people were in costume and some paid at the door in cash, so it's not definitive."

Cesare nudged closer to her and eased his snout onto her lap. He eyed her list drowsily, probably hoping it was a grocery list full of red meat, cheese, yogurt, and peanut butter.

"Based on their Facebook accounts, Diana and Aria seem to have been at a yoga meditation retreat in the Berkshires the weekend of the Carnevale ball. Very New Age-y, all total nonsense of course." Luciano nodded in agreement. "They took lots of photos of themselves in tight spandex, all time stamped, so I can probably rule them out from attending the ball. Now, Teri"—her voice rose, and Luciano perked up as if this could be important—"was supposed to go, but stayed home with the flu. Her husband and kids definitely attended the ball—but Marion was in charge of the ticket sales and she tells me they bought their tickets with a credit card. So Teri could have paid cash and slipped in and they'd never know. And she could have been in cahoots with Marie, who is after all her aunt. And Marie did bump Greta."

Rita frowned. "But the poison was in Julia's drink, not Greta's."

With a sigh, she circled Teri's name and wrote next to it, "working with Marie?" in red pen.

Rita went back to skimming the list of participants in the foraging expedition. She crossed herself, Rose and Calvino off the list. She was about to cross Orlando off, too, but then she thought about that night in the woods. What if Orlando had found out Greta's horrible secret, and what if that secret had turned him against her?

But no matter what it was, wouldn't he just have called off the wedding instead of killing her?

She put a faint red line under Orlando's name, realizing with a sinking heart that she could not eliminate him. He certainly was at both the foraging expedition and the ball, and he could have lied when he said he hadn't been the one to give Julia the poisoned wine.

"Now Bianca," she said to Luciano, "had a strong motive and actually threatened to kill Greta."

She couldn't bring herself to say it out loud, but she admitted the possibility by underlining Bianca's name twice.

"Then there's Jack," she said. "He was on the foraging expedition, but there's no evidence he was at the ball, although I can't say for sure he wasn't. But I can't see he'd have a motive anyhow."

"That leaves Viola"—she underlined Viola's name three times, then put an exclamation point after it—"who had a definite motive and has already been shown to have a criminal mind. And she was at the ball—Orlando confirmed it—and the foraging expedition, obviously. Plus, she's an expert in poisons."

Luciano barked.

"She's almost too obvious, isn't she?" Rita agreed with him. "And perhaps I am biased against her."

Her eyes fell to the bottom of the list. "And then Luca and McKenzie. McKenzie has a motive, and her anger is white-hot. But does she know anything about poisons....?"

Rita picked up the phone. "Perhaps I should talk to an actual human," she said to Luciano and Cesare apologetically as she dialed her sister's number.

"Yes?" Her twin's voice was uncharacteristically faint.

"This connection's terrible," Rita said. "I can hardly hear you."

"Shhh. I'm on Viola's trail, and she's about to walk past my car. She just came out of the gastroenterologist."

"What?"

"I know. The woman's got serious digestive issues. I trailed her to the grocery store, and she was really stocking up on Metamucil."

Rita sighed. "No, I mean—why are you following her?"

"To get some dirt on her," Rose said impatiently. Suddenly, her voice sounded very British. "Oh, hello, love—yes, I'd love a new jumper, maybe in aubergine. Could you order it from the catalogue? Whew—okay, she's gone."

"Who orders sweaters from a parked car?"

"Well, I'm sure you'd think of something better," Rose huffed. "But then you're not helping me, are you? Oh, hold on—she's on the move. I'm slipping in behind her. She's headed up Main Street, probably going home. She's off work today."

"Are we still meeting for coffee at the Sunshine Café?"

The sisters met up most Wednesday afternoons at the Sunshine Café, especially now that Rita was a silent partner in the business and ate free for life.

"No." Rose sounded annoyed. "But if you want to meet up, meet me down the block from Viola's house, wearing something totally uncharacteristic, and bring the dogs—no, better yet, bring Gina's schnauzer. Piddles is less distinctive."

Chapter Twenty-Two

A half an hour later, Rita and Rose met around the corner from Viola's house. Rose looked Rita up and down, zeroing in on her skintight fuchsia hoodie emblazoned with "Juicy" in sequins, which Rita had "borrowed" from Gina. Perched at an alarming angle on Rita's bushy black hair was a matching fuchsia fascinator, a castoff from last year's St. Vincent's Ladies' Auxiliary Tea whose arching curlicues made it look as though Rita's head were a fireworks launch pad.

"Well," Rose said, "you *do* look different. Kind of like an Italian Camilla, Duchess of Cornwall, blown up to Rita size and stuffed into Kim Kardashian's clothing."

"Sal," Rita huffed, "said I looked like a cross between Sofia Loren and Kate Middleton."

She knew, of course, that part of the reason he said that was because he was angling for lasagna tonight, but there was no need to tell her smug sister as much. After all, she wouldn't be wearing this ridiculous get-up if it weren't for the fact that Rose had been cavorting in her birthday suit in a client's hot tub.

With Piddles in tow, the sisters rounded the corner, and Viola's house came into view. It was a forbidding, turreted stone manse, surrounded by a low stone wall. It had always reminded Rita of Sleeping Beauty's castle. The row of yew bushes beneath the mullioned front windows, with their bright red poisonous berries, and the gnarled, twisted Japanese pine tree in the front yard did nothing to dispel the illusion. And then of course, there was the mansion's occupant, who had always reminded Rita a bit of the Wicked Witch, even more so now that she knew Viola was blackmailing half the town.

"I haven't been able to see a thing inside," Rose said in a low voice. "I think she has tinted windows, kind of like hit men and drug dealers have on their cars. But she did open the door once and let out a black cat."

Somehow, Viola's choice of pet did not surprise Rita in the least. She wondered if it had glowing green eyes and was named Lucifer.

"What else have you learned?" Rita asked as Piddles relieved himself against a lamppost.

"She's a terrible driver, has spring allergies, has terrible digestion, drinks her coffee black, orders only salads from the Sunshine Café, always leaves an exact fifteen percent tip, calculated to the penny, and appears to have no friends and no social life."

None of that surprised Rita. She suddenly felt very pleased that she took her coffee with cream and three lumps of sugar; always ordered the chicken salad on a croissant at the Sunshine Café, with a huge slab of chocolate cake for dessert; tipped generously; and surrounded herself with family (wayward as some of them might be), friends, co-workers, and all manner of acquaintances, partners in crime, and co-conspirators from the quilting circle, the funeral choir, and the ladies' auxiliary.

"But," Rose added, suddenly brightening, "I also discovered that Viola drives all the way to Poughkeepsie on secret trips to buy steamy paperback romance novels—and I mean *steamy*—and love potions from a Puerto Rican *botanica*."

Rita's mouth fell open.

"Yup," Rose said happily, "like Bring Back My Man purple scented candles and this green gooey shampoo that smells terrible and is a mixture of some Amazon jungle plant and blood from the heart of some bird that mates for life. She's supposed to mix that into Orlando's shampoo."

Rita wanted to feel some kind of triumph or joy or mirth, but somehow she found it more tragic than funny. To her surprise, she actually pitied Viola.

They were nearing the house now, causing Rose to suddenly switch to a bad Australian accent.

"Now, Down Under, mate," Rose was saying, sounding a little like Rosie O'Donnell trying to imitate Crocodile Dundee, "a house like this is just a hovel. We're dripping with mining money. We've got a waterfront mansion in Sydney, a house in Tasmania, and one in wine country. Plus, a ranch with ten thousand sheep and some kangaroos. This here house might be okay for the stable boy."

Piddles decided to do his business right in front of Viola's stone wall.

"*Bravo*, Piddles!" Rita whispered, patting him gently, as she very slowly leaned down to pick up after him. She took the opportunity to peer over the wall, pretending to admire the stonework. She thought she saw a flash of something bright in the window at the top of the turret. Was Viola watching them with binoculars?

Who was spying on whom?

The thought made Rita's blood run cold. She was suddenly very afraid for her sister.

"Yes," Rita said, playing the part of the loud, proud American cousin, "but you have Marmite, wildfires, and those bellowing digeridoos, and we have autumn colors, cannoli, and world-class summer stock theater." Rita lowered her voice and nudged her sister. "*Andiamo*," she hissed. "I think she's watching."

The two sisters walked briskly down the block, continuing their animated discussion of which was better—Australia or the Hudson Valley. When they finally reached the end of the block and turned down a charming lane lined with white picket fences and snug wooden bungalows, Rose finally dropped the act.

"Are you sure she was watching?"

For once, Rose's confidence seemed to have deserted her.

"I'm almost positive," Rita said.

"Do you think she killed Greta?"

Rose sounded both hopeful and scared. Rita knew her sister well enough to know what she was thinking. If

Viola had killed Greta, that might mean they could put her behind bars before she could terrorize Rose any further. On the other hand, it also meant Viola was perfectly capable of killing Rose, too.

"I don't know," Rita said. "She's crazy about Orlando—that's for sure. And passion is a powerful motive. She certainly had the opportunity, too. As the judge for the competition, she was walking around to everyone's cook station, including Greta's. And she knew more about poisoned foraged foods than anyone."

"But?"

"I don't think she'd have been sloppy enough to have poisoned Julia by accident."

"Maybe there are two different killers on the loose. Maybe someone wanted Julia dead and failed. And then Viola killed Greta. Or maybe Julia poisoned *herself* to throw everyone off track and then poisoned Greta. Maybe *she* was in love with Orlando...or wanted revenge over something that happened a long time ago."

Rita shook her head. "I would never believe Julia to be a killer, plus she wasn't even on the foraging expedition. No, my money's on Viola,"—she starting ticking off each one on her fingers—"McKenzie, who had a white-hot hatred of Greta and was at both the Carnevale ball and St. Vincent's; Teri, whose family's land abuts the winery and would be negatively impacted by the expansion, who was definitely at the foraging expedition and could have been at the ball, and is possibly in cahoots with her aunt, Orlando's ex-wife Marie; or...."

Rita trailed off. Her throat was dry, her hands clammy.

"Or?" Rose said sharply.

"Bianca."

Rose gasped. "Bianca? You've known her since she was a girl."

"I know," Rita said grimly. "But I can't ignore the fact that she was the one person who said she wanted Greta dead, who was definitely in close proximity to Greta both at the ball and at the foraging event, and who knows Greta intimately and can probably predict her every move."

"Have you told Gina this?"

"No—and if you know what's good for you, you won't either."

Chapter Twenty-Three

A heavy fog rose off the river like some sort of shape-shifting otherworldly being, its ghostly tentacles reaching out into every far-flung hollow and hamlet, encircling the mountains in an uneasy embrace.

"A good day for a murder," Sam said darkly when Rita called to tell her that she and Calvino were postponing their fact-finding trip to Binghampton until the fog cleared. "There better be one, because at the moment the top story we're looking at is 'Fog Envelopes Valley.' Which everyone kind of, like, already knows."

"Art Jones is very entertaining," Rita said, trying to console Sam. Art was the weatherman on the local TV station, and he was well known for his polka dot bow ties, horrible puns, and droll humor. "I'm sure he'll provide some great quotes while trying to explain what has caused this infernal fog. And maybe we can trot out some story about *The Legend of Sleepy Hollow*."

It was a matter of some pride in Morris County that Washington Irving had based the *Legend of Sleepy Hollow* on Acorn Hollow, even if those perfidious yuppies in

Tarrytown, further south, tried to claim that distinction for themselves.

"And there was that never-solved murder," Rita reminded Sam, "that occurred in the sixties during a pea-soup fog just like this, right after a high school production of the *Legend*."

Rita promised to whip her old notes about the cold case into a story by six, and suggested that Ana, their teenaged intern, contact Art for a story. Before long, Sam was making noises suggesting she was moderately appeased and rang off.

"Phew," Rita said to Luciano and Cesare, who had been hovering at her feet hopefully. She winked at them as she flung open the refrigerator and tossed some diced prosciutto into their bowls. "Good thing I already wrote the story months ago and it's saved on my computer."

She opened her laptop, typed up an email to Sam, attached the story, and scheduled her email to be sent at 5:59 p.m. Sam secretly enjoyed the drama of almost-missed deadlines and late breaking news, and Rita would hate to spoil her fun.

"Now," she said to her dogs, as she snatched her jacket and her keys, "on to the real investigating—and to consulting the wisest living person in all of Acorn Hollow."

Since Rita could barely see two feet in front of her, she relied on Luciano and Cesare to guide her through the gaps in the higgly-piggly rows of molding headstones marking the graves of Acorn Hollow's earliest settlers, the dour, pious Dutch farmers of New Amsterdam, over the brow of the hill into a later section of granite monuments inscribed with flowery, sentimental tributes to the deceased in beautiful Italian, and then into a midcentury, more democratic hodgepodge of tombs and gravestones. Their yelps of anticipation grew louder until they halted suddenly, two familiar black buttoned-up boots peeking through the swirling mist.

A crackly voice with rich, plummy vowels cut through the gloom. "Well, don't drop her in my lap, boys. I'm fragile, you know."

Rita reached out blindly and patted the cold marble slab until she clasped a tiny, bird-boned hand. "Hello, Emma."

Rita was the only person in Acorn Hollow who had the temerity to call her Emma. Intimidated by her great age, her piercing dark eyes, her all-black attire (always accented by a hint of red, which put people uncomfortably in mind of a black widow spider), and her habit of reading the newspaper to her three deceased husbands in the cemetery, everyone called her The Widow Schmalzgruben. The name was typically said with a knowing glance, and often a shiver, for the circumstances surrounding her second and third husbands' deaths had always been a bit murky.

But she was Rita's great friend and confidant—and one of her superfans. The widow read her articles religiously and was often a great source of information, not to mention a font of wisdom and insight. She had not lived more than a century for nothing.

And yet, in spite of her great age, she possessed surprising youth and vitality. Her one concession to old age had been trading in her black limousine for a golf cart, and that was only after she had accidentally driven the limo through the post office's brand-new glass façade.

"Mind if I sit with you?" Rita asked, though she already knew the answer.

"Be my guest, dear. I was just reading your article on the tango lessons to Thomas, here. He was quite the dancer, you know. We used to dance every Saturday night at the Elks' Club. And what a lovely picture of Gina and Matt! It's a pity I don't see them as a couple."

Rita's heart sank; the widow was usually right about these things.

The tiny bird-boned hand reached out and squeezed Rita's with surprising strength. "It's in the eyes, dear. Gina is not really looking at him. She's looking across the room at someone else."

"Jack," Rita said miserably. "A nice kid, but just that—a kid. Boundless enthusiasm, but no culture and no sense."

The widow laughed. "My Thomas was six years younger than me. And what fun we had!" She chuckled. "But that's not why you're here—to get my views on Gina and her latest paramour. My bet would be that murder is probably what's on your mind—specifically Greta's."

Rita plopped down on the marble slab. It was damp, cold, and clammy. "Well?" she said as she felt two lumps of fur nestle on top of her feet. "What do you think?"

"Well, who stands most to gain from her death—or lose the most if she stays alive? And mind you, I don't just mean financially. Psychology plays a big role in murder. To whom did she represent some kind of threat—to their relationships, their loved ones, or their sense of self?"

"Bianca," Rita said in a hoarse whisper. "She said Greta was just a gold-digger, but it was more than that, I think. I think Greta threatened her close relationship with her father. Teri—Greta's expansion plans for the winery would create a nuisance for her family and their farm. And Viola—she was in love with Orlando."

"But," the widow countered, "Viola never killed Marie."

"No, but maybe it seemed hopeless when he was married to Marie, but then when he was divorced, she dared to dream...."

"Well, if she did," the widow said sharply, "she was a fool. Anyone with eyes could see that he had no interest in a dried-up prune like her. But then, there's no shortage of foolishness in this world—or people whose foolishness gets them into trouble. If I had a nickel for every woman in Acorn Hollow—most of them now in this cemetery—who made a fool of herself over a man, I'd be a rich woman indeed."

Rita smiled. Even if every woman who had ever lived in Acorn Hollow was a fool, this would add up to less than a thousand dollars, given the town's diminutive size.

"Greta also represented a threat to McKenzie, I suppose," Rita said, "although the threat was rather past. According to Gina, Greta tried to get McKenzie's mom ousted as head librarian and then tried to sic the health inspectors on the Sunshine Café, claiming there was a bug in her soup, which McKenzie had made."

"There probably was a bug. I stopped going to the Sunshine Café forty years ago, when a mouse scurried over my foot." The widow cackled merrily. "That Greta seems like the kind who always has a bee in her bonnet, one of those holier-than-thou types. They always come to a bad end, though. In my day, there was Maryanne the librarian, who railed against smutty books, abhorred dancing, and would blacklist you from the library for the slightest infraction, but then wound up in the family way—and it turned out the father was the married preacher! The two of them got run out of town on a rail, ended up as carnival workers, and their little girl got polio and died. Then he left her for a contortionist."

"How dreadful!"

"Those were the days." A sigh emanated out of the gloom. The mist parted just enough for Rita to catch a glimpse of the widow's snow-white bun and the back of her starched black, high-necked collar. "There's no controversy now—everyone, even kids, reads smutty books; nothing's banned, except of course the circus; and running off with someone else's husband is just how women get husband number two. It's all really quite boring."

"Well," Rita said, "until someone ends up dead."

"Mmmm, yes—there is still murder." The widow sounded almost happy about that.

Rita reached down to pet Luciano and Cesare. "Do you think there's any chance it could be Orlando?"

"Oh, definitely," the widow said. "There probably isn't a married person in town who hasn't contemplated

murdering their spouse at some point. I know I did."
The widow cackled. "Which isn't to say I killed any of
my husbands—or that I didn't."

Rita attempted to laugh, but it came out as an uneasy
chuckle.

"You could ask Orlando now," the widow said. Her
wrinkled visage came into faded view, peeking through
the mist like a ghostly apparition. Rita could finally see
what the widow had selected as the day's red accent: a
red ribbon wound round her neck. In the center, just
above her high-necked collar, resting on her Adam's
apple, was a memento mori, a glass bauble containing a
lock of hair from her mother, who had perished from
the Spanish Flu. The hair was twisted into the shape of a
flower.

"He's here," the widow said, "visiting Greta's grave.
Four rows down and about two hundred yards over."

Rita spun around, but other than the ghostly
silhouette of a few trees, she couldn't make out a thing.
"He is? How can you tell?"

"Oh, I have very keen eyesight," the widow said. "As
I used to tell the children when I was a schoolteacher, I
have eyes on the back of my head. I see everything. I
know everything."

Despite the fact that they were friends, the widow's
words sent a chill down Rita's spine.

Chapter Twenty-Four

Luciano and Cesare guided her down the hill, her hands splayed out in front of her, her fingertips occasionally brushing over a rough-hewn stone marker or springy clump of mold. She counted out the four rows of tombstones, then tugged her dogs to the left. When she had gone at least one hundred yards, she began to call out, "Orlando! Orlando!"

At first, there was no answer, other than the eerie tapping of a hollow branch against a tombstone and the sloshing of eight paws and two rain boots on the waterlogged grass.

At last, she heard a faint response, "Who's there?"

"Rita!" she cried. "Rita Calabrese! Say something more so I can follow the sound of your voice."

He began singing "*E Lucevan Le Stelle*" from *Tosca*, tentatively at first, then more powerfully. His voice was heavy with emotion; standing by the grave of his beloved Greta, he probably felt more alone than ever.

"*Che voce bello!*" Rita marveled as she approached. There was a darker patch in the fog ahead, and it slowly morphed into the shape of a man. "I didn't know you could sing. Why, you should join our funeral choir!"

"I would find it too depressing," he said apologetically. "Especially now."

She took another step, and she was now so close to him, she could hear him breathing. In another step, his craggy features emerged from the miasma. Tears streaming down his face, his fists balled up, he was looking down at the large gray marker he had chosen for Greta. A blank slate, there was nothing carved on it yet. The earth was soft and springy beneath their feet; the cemetery had not yet laid new sod down, and they were standing on a mound of freshly dug earth.

"I thought this was my new beginning," he said softly, "but it ended before it even began. She was so young—too young."

Looking at him, she could scarcely believe him capable of killing Greta. He didn't look guilty so much as in pain.

He turned to look at her and without even bothering to wipe away his tears, asked, "Will you help me find the *stronzo* who did this, Rita? You're the only one I trust."

"I'm already on the case, I assure you." She reached out and squeezed his arm. "But to solve this, you're going to need to tell me everything you know."

When he didn't respond, she applied a little more pressure and said, "*Tutto, assolutamento tutto.*"

She felt him flinch slightly.

"I know," she said slowly, "that you were being blackmailed, but I don't know why. The reason could be an important clue."

"I can tell you, but I can't see how it's related. A while ago, my Uncle Flavio got in trouble. He owed, uh, some gentlemen—"

"By some gentlemen, you mean *La Cosa Nostra?*" Rita used the Italian name for the mob, lest someone be listening...and she rather suspected the widow was.

He nodded slowly. "He owed them some money and if he didn't pay up, they'd, you know"—he drew a finger across his neck— "so I helped him out."

"Helped him how?"

"I paid his debt."

"Is that a crime?"

"Probably. Maybe. I mean, it could look like a crime—I paid a lot of money to some lowlife with no paperwork. People might get the wrong idea of what it was for."

Rita's heart went out to him. All he had done was save the life and reputation of a family member, and Viola had somehow turned this act of generosity into a sword of Damocles.

"And that's it?"

"That's it. I swear. So, you see, I can't see how that could have spiraled into Greta's murder. They had no reason to go after me. I paid the debt and that was it."

Rita took a deep breath and steeled herself for her next question. "And what about Greta? Why was she being blackmailed?"

He turned to stare at her. "Blackmailed? Greta? You must be joking."

"I'm not."

If he had discovered Greta's secret, Rita thought, he certainly hid it well.

"Mi *dispiace*, Rita, but I haven't the faintest idea."

Orlando invited Rita back to the winery to pore through Greta's papers in the hopes of finding some clue, but Rita came up empty-handed. Either the police had already removed everything of interest, or Greta had destroyed the blackmailer's missives.

An alternative, much darker theory popped into Rita's head. "Orlando," she said, "has Viola been in here?"

"Viola? Yes, I think she tidied up Greta's office a bit. You know Viola—she always likes things ship-shape and she is always so helpful."

Yes, Rita thought, but Viola helps no one so much as herself. And the most helpful thing Viola could have done for herself is to destroy the evidence of blackmail.

Trying to sound casual, Rita asked, "Before or after the police arrived?"

A slight frown crossed Orlando's face. "After, of course. She showed the police in here and then stayed behind afterwards to tidy up."

Rita could just imagine a scenario in which Viola was able to distract the police long enough to snatch the offending letter and conceal it.

"Well, then," Rita said, straightening up and shutting the last drawer, "there's nothing to be found here. Now, tell me, before I go, does Teri Bertinelli have a weakness for anything in particular?"

"Tiramisu. Before the disagreement about the winery expansion, she and her husband used to come almost every Saturday night for dinner, and they always ordered the tiramisu."

"Excellent! Then I'll take a whole tiramisu to go."

Rita left her car in the winery parking lot. She walked briskly to the small wooden gate to the Bertinellis' property, popped the latch, and then walked down the dappled dirt lane past pear trees just beginning to bud and dark furrowed vegetable beds soon to be planted, to a rustic country farmhouse. It was charmingly old-fashioned, with a wraparound porch, big porch swing, and flower boxes beneath all the windows. The first daffodils were just bursting forth, there were hens pecking their way through the surrounding yard, and an orange tabby cat was curled up napping on the mat by the front door.

Rita pressed the buzzer and waited until a barefoot Teri answered the door, a little white terrier close at her heels. She clearly had not expected to see Rita.

"Oh!" was initially all she said. Then her eyes flew to the glistening, cocoa-dusted tiramisu in Rita's hands. "Oh—what a lovely tiramisu. I mean, oh—where are my manners? Hello, Rita—I mean, Mrs. Calabrese."

She dried her wet hands on her apron, which hung limply from her tiny waist, and reached out to shake Rita's hand.

Rita and Teri did not know each other well—not at all, really—but Rita had known her mother, Antonella, a sprightly old woman who had sung—or as Sal would say, "wailed"—in the funeral choir with Rita. When Antonella had died, the choir's harmony improved, but Rita felt that something had been lost.

"Thank you for the lovely card you sent when *mamma* died, and the lasagna."

"It was *niente*, trust me. Your mother was such a stalwart member of the funeral choir. And such a ball of energy! Quite an inspiration to us all."

Rita put one foot in the door and leaned her body forward slightly, so that the fulcrum was over the threshold. In her experience, the first and most crucial step to gaining entrance to anyone's home was to make it seem quite natural, even inevitable, and she was not beyond subtle physical intimidation.

"I wanted to check in and see how you are doing," Rita said, "you know, after the funeral. Because sometimes that's the hardest part, after everyone has departed. And I thought perhaps we could have a nice chat over some coffee and tiramisu."

Rita could sense Teri was wavering.

"Oh—I thought you might be here about a story."

Accidenti! Teri had seen right through her.

"Well, we can talk about the winery expansion controversy if you like." Rita chose her words carefully. "I was thinking of doing a story about it, although perhaps it's a bit of a moot point now. Orlando says he's not sure if he feels like going ahead now that Greta's gone."

"Really?" Teri looked relieved beyond measure. "That would be wonderful news! Although"—she looked down and tried to look contrite—"the circumstances are, of course, terrible."

"Yes, but as with so many things in life, there is a silver lining...."

Rita took another step forward so both feet were now firmly planted across the threshold. She held out the tiramisu, so that Teri would have no choice but to accept it.

Teri's delicate little fingers were just curving around the box when suddenly a dark, menacing shape appeared in the back of the hallway.

"Rita," screeched a sharp voice that sounded like nails on a chalkboard.

"Marie."

"Thank you for the lovely tiramisu," Marie said, although she sounded anything but thankful. "My niece and I would love to have you in, but you'll have to take a raincheck. Teri and I are meeting with our lawyer and"— she tapped her watch—"he charges by the minute."

Teri smiled apologetically, and Rita stepped back onto the porch. "Lawyers," Rita said. "Yes, they are expensive. But if this is about the winery expansion, perhaps they are not needed."

Marie did not rise to the bait. She would neither confirm nor deny exactly what they needed this particular lawyer for—if, in fact, the lawyer even existed. Rita could imagine that Marie would invent any manner of excuse to keep her niece from speaking to Rita. She was sure Marie would hiss something like "loose lips sink ships" to Teri the moment the door was slammed shut in Rita's face.

"Good-bye, Rita," Marie said. "Now, come along, Teri."

Rita felt dejected. She had lost one delicious tiramisu and gained precious little information, other than that Teri and Marie were indeed close—and possibly plotting some legal action against Orlando...or someone else.

Rita stormed back to her car in high dudgeon.

"Poor Orlando," she muttered as she roared out of the parking lot, "after Marie, he certainly deserved better."

Chapter Twenty-Five

The fog had cleared by morning but, by the time Rita was an hour into her road trip with Calvino, she almost wished it hadn't. Her companion was as rude, crude, uncouth, and loud-mouthed as ever, and he was just warming up.

"Get a load of this," he shouted, smacking the *Morris County Gazette* and shaking his head in righteous indignation. " 'One Confused Dude' wrote in again. You remember him, right? The young guy trying to date the cougar?"

Rita shot him an icy glare. "Not a cougar, Calvino. A mature woman."

"Whatever." He shrugged. "Anyway, he actually took The Dude's terrible advice to be 'the friend.' And guess what? It backfired. Now the cougar's using him to get close to two different guys—apparently, she wants a pair and a spare. First, she wants him to befriend The Bachelor—you know, that guy from the tango class that all the girls are gaga over—and talk her up to him. Then, she wants him to ask out this other chick who's the girlfriend of some la-di-dah restaurant owner—probably a friend of Dorothy, know what I mean?—so she can swoop in and get him."

He threw down the paper in disgust. "Way to go, Dude."

Interesting, Rita thought. So someone has her eye on both Matt Peruzzi and Luca Della Rosa. And that someone, she suspected, was Bianca. She'd seen how Bianca had angled to dance with Matt at the tango lesson and lusted after Luca on the foraging expedition.

Well, she thought, much as I love Bianca, she'll have to look elsewhere for a partner. Luca was already taken and, if Rita had her way, Matt would be soon, too—by Gina.

"Hey, ease up the lead foot, there, Rita."

Calvino's voice startled Rita and she looked up in time to see that her speedometer was shooting past eighty.

"I'm all for fast cars and fast women," Calvino said, "but we're coming up to a speed trap."

Rita eased off the gas pedal. "How could you possibly know that?"

"Oh, I've got this app, see? It tracks all the speed traps in real time."

"I think that's illegal, Calvino."

"Why? It forces me to drive slower and that's a good thing, right?"

Rita tightened her grip on the steering wheel. "So what was The Dude's response?"

" 'Dear 'Confused,'" Calvino read, his voice dripping with derision and disbelief, " 'you should reconsider whether you even want this chick. She seems like a happy homewrecker. Sure, today she wants you to break up the restaurant owner's relationship, but what about tomorrow when you're together? Plus, she can't even decide which guy she wants. She sounds like a fruitcake. My advice? Find someone your own age who wants to be with you and is less of a nutcase.'"

"Well, what's wrong with that?" Rita said. It actually seemed like rather sound advice, if crudely delivered, although she was a little uncomfortable with the aspersions cast on Bianca's character. But then, perhaps Rita had a bit of a blind spot where Bianca was concerned.

"Nothing," Calvino said, "except he should have said that in the first place. And he should admit he was wrong the first time!"

"Oh, but this column is called 'Ask a Dude,'" Rita said with a laugh, " 'Not Ask a Woman.' Men don't usually admit they're wrong."

Calvino grunted and folded his arms over his chest. He looked out at the patchwork of fields and forests that spread as far as the eye could see. For the first time that morning, he was actually silent.

"Are you ready to admit you were wrong?" Rita said gently. "To ask for Concetta's forgiveness? To find out what self-actualized means to her and help her get self-actualized?"

Calvino grunted again.

Rita asked, "Is that cave man for yes or for no?"

"It means I'll think about it. But it's ridiculous, you know. It's just these silly books that put these silly ideas in her head. She's happy, she just doesn't know it!"

"And you do?"

"Absolutely."

"Well," Rita said, "even if that's true, would you rather be right or happy?"

Instead of answering directly, Calvino balled his fists up in fury, pounded them on his lap, and said, "I just don't want to turn into a namby-pamby softie like The Dude."

"Really? It might surprise you to find out who The Dude actually is."

"Try me."

"The Dude is none other," she said, "than your favorite, very manly and definitely not gay, cousin."

It seemed as if a whole hour had passed before Calvino picked his jaw up off the floor. "No," he just kept saying. "Sal wouldn't—he couldn't. All that sappy crap? No, it couldn't be. Plus, he can't even write. A columnist? Never."

"Trust me, Calvino. I was just as surprised as you when I found out."

"He kept it a secret from you?"

"Well, he wasn't sure I would approve. See, Calvino? It just goes to show that no one knows their spouse as well as they think they do."

She suddenly thought of Orlando, standing beside Greta's grave, looking shocked and bewildered that Greta, too, harbored some kind of secret—a secret Greta was so anxious to keep that she had succumbed to blackmail.

"And," Rita said, brushing the thought away, "it just goes to show that lots of us—even men—feel the need to be self-actualized at some point."

"Huh." Calvino was looking at her like she was speaking ancient Greek. He massaged his temples and shook his head back and forth vigorously as if to wipe his memory clean of this bewildering conversation. "So, what's the plan when we get to Binghampton?"

"Ah—the plan." She, too, felt rather relieved to be back in familiar territory and leave the counseling session behind. "Well, Julia Simms gave me the names of Greta's foster parents, but they are nowhere to be found. Most likely, they passed away. So that's a dead end. But two of the three women who were childhood friends of theirs—who got the butterfly tattoo when Jenny Farfalle died—are still around."

"What happened to the other one?"

"Lung cancer."

"Jeez."

"So that leaves us with Katie O'Hara, who's a dentist, and Susie Balistreri, who specializes in tattoo removal."

"So we're just gonna walk in and say 'hey, what do you know about this dead chick, Greta?' "

"No. You're due for a teeth cleaning and"—she reached out a finger and drew up Calvino's ratty T-shirt, revealing a Cupid tattoo emblazoned with 'Denise' – "you are going to be an enthusiastic client of Susie's, eager to remove all evidence of your relationship with Denise in your quest to win back Concetta."

Despite his bulk, Calvino seemed to shrink into the passenger seat.

"Although," she said, "you can always back out at the last moment—after I get the scoop."

Chapter Twenty-Six

The waiting room for the dentist's office was stark white and filled with patients who looked just as terrified as Calvino.

"Where's your sense of morals?" Calvino muttered in Rita's ear as she filled out the paperwork. "You can't claim I'm Sal. That's insurance fraud."

Rita shrugged. "Sal hasn't been to the dentist in the last two years, so he's long overdue for a cleaning. The insurance company is making boatloads of money off of us. Besides, think about the greater good. We're solving a murder. Don't you care about what happened to Greta?"

"Yeah," Calvino said, watching in horror as a large tropical fish with razor-sharp teeth devoured a smaller fish in the aquarium behind them. It was like watching the Nature Channel. "But I also care about what happens to *me* once I get in the chair. I mean, look how they treat the *fish*."

"*Non preoccupare*," Rita murmured reassuringly. "Your loving wife will be by your side while they drill and polish your pearly whites."

"Huh?"

"Well, if you're Sal, then I'm your wife."

"Oh, Lord help me."

The receptionist called Sal's name, and Rita nudged Calvino.

"That's you," she hissed. "*Andiamo*."

She placed one hand on the small of his back and propelled him forwards. "Just think," she muttered, "about how great your teeth will look when you finally see Concetta."

The dental hygienist stopped her gently as they fell in behind her. "I'm sorry, ma'am, but the only time we allow a loved one to accompany another patient is when the patient is a child."

Rita shot the woman a severe look over her glasses. "And your point?"

The woman frowned and said nothing.

"Have you been married?" Rita asked.

"No."

"Ah—well if you had, then you'd know that having a husband is pretty much like having a child. Worse, actually, especially when it comes to the dentist."

Rita could tell that the hygienist was struggling to come up with a suitable retort, as she screwed up her pert little nose and thin fish lips. But finding none, she let out an exasperated sigh and ushered them both in.

Rita smiled beatifically all through Calvino's cleaning, murmuring pleasantly every time a gargled "You owe me big time" or "I'm gonna kill you, Rita" escaped Calvino's lips.

When Dr. O'Hara finally made an appearance, Rita waited to pounce until after the good dentist had poked and prodded each of Calvino's teeth, found two cavities, and recommended a root canal.

"I always tell him," Rita clucked, "to take better care of his teeth. But does he listen? No. He's always sneaking cannoli, *struffoli*, biscotti, tiramisu—"

"And who makes all of these desserts?" Dr. O'Hara asked. She was a pleasantly plump woman with big blue eyes and blue-rimmed square glasses. Unlike her childhood friend Greta, she actually looked as though she were pushing fifty.

"Oh"—Rita blushed—"well, that would be me."

"Ah—so the solution's simple. Stop baking."

"Oh, well, I—"

Dr. O'Hara wagged a finger and stopped Rita in mid-flow. "No ifs, ands, or buts. The spouse is usually part of the problem—and the solution."

Flummoxed and completely unused to being caught up short like that, Rita could think of nothing to say. After a moment, she recovered and said, "The problem is that baking is like therapy for me. And I've just been so sad lately, ever since my good friend Peggy Wisniewski died. Well, that's a nice way of saying it—she was murdered, actually."

Dr. O'Hara suddenly lost interest in Calvino's teeth. She abruptly put her instruments on the tray beside her.

Pressing her advantage, Rita said, "That's why we're here, you see. I wanted to look up her family and give them my condolences. Of course, I'm not quite sure how to find them. Might I ask when you graduated from high school? I was hoping you might know her."

"Nineteen eighty-eight," Dr. O'Hara said mechanically, with a faraway look in her eye. Rita noticed that she turned her wrist slightly and snuck a look at the tiny blue butterfly tattoo there before pulling her sleeve over it hastily. "I knew her a bit in high school," she said, "but we drifted apart afterwards. I haven't seen her in decades. Last I heard she married a Canadian."

Rita shook her head sadly. "That didn't last unfortunately. She was set to be marrying a winery owner in the Hudson Valley next month, but now, well....He's heartbroken."

They were silent for a moment, and Calvino shifted uncomfortably in the dentist's chair.

"Tell me," Rita said, "what was she like as a teenager?"

Dr. O'Hara hesitated a moment. Rita could tell she was choosing her words carefully.

"Pretty," the dentist said finally, "and very popular. With a flair for the dramatic." She picked up her drill and brandished it in the air. "And that's about all I can recall."

Chapter Twenty-Seven

Fortunately, Susie Balistreri, the tattoo removal artist, was as loquacious as Katie O'Hara was reticent. "I go by Suze now," she said when Rita made the mistake of asking for Susie. "It fits my personality a whole lot better, know what I mean?"

Rita was not sure what was the polite response, although she tended to agree. Susie sounded like some nice pigtailed girl who sold Girl Scout cookies and did cartwheels in the lawn; Suze sounded more like the woman before her, who was short and squat, with a salt-and-pepper buzz cut, a Marilyn Manson T-shirt across her flat chest and Doc Martens on her feet, and her fingernails painted black.

"Yup," Calvino blurted out. His lip was still fat from the novacaine and he talked with a bit of a lisp. "I sure do."

Suze pushed Calvino down into a chair. "Now, let's see what we've got here."

Without any niceties, she pulled up both his sleeves. Calvino reacted by tugging nervously at his sleeves and shying away, as if he'd been violated.

Suze whistled. "Lots of tats. So, which one are we taking off today? Starting to take off, that is—it'll take six to eight sessions to get it off completely."

Calvino didn't respond. Instead, his eyes darted around the parlor, inspecting every nook and cranny.

"Don't worry," she said, slugging him on the arm. "We just passed our health inspection last month. We're clean as a whistle and do everything by the book. We're the best tattoo removal place in the state. I even have a contract with the Pen." She laughed. "Too bad you're not a prisoner. Then I'd take them off for free and send the bill to the governor. But don't worry; I'll get you a discount. Are you a vet? AARP member?"

"Both," Calvino said weakly.

"See? You just got yourself a ten percent discount. I'll make it a fifteen percent volume discount if you do more than three today. Plus, keep in mind I'm a whiz at not only removal, but editing. Yup, I do that too. Like one lady, she was dating a Bryan, see? But then he knocked her up and left her broke and with a busted lip. So she wanted the tat removed but didn't know if she could stand the pain, so I said, hey, I've got a real nice client named Ryan I could set you up with and then we'd only need to get rid of the 'B.' I didn't tell her, 'course, that Ryan was one of those freebie clients from the Pen."

Rita was aghast. "You set her up with a prisoner?"

"Ex-prisoner." Suze rolled her eyes at Rita as if she were the most unreasonable, intolerant person ever. "He only did two years' hard time. He was a nice guy—he got out early for good behavior. And now they're married and have three kids."

Calvino nodded as if this whole story made sense. "Wow," he said, "and she only had to remove one letter."

Rita cleared her throat loudly.

"Oh," Calvino said, "so I need to remove this Denise tattoo."

His eyes moistened, and he suddenly became very solemn. "Because there's only one woman for me. And that's Concetta."

Suze handed Calvino a raft of paperwork. While Calvino was flipping through it and dutifully signing every form, Rita asked Suze, "Did you grow up here?"

Suze rolled her eyes. "Unfortunately."

"Good—you see, I've been trying to find someone who knows Peggy Wisniewski. I was hoping to offer my condolences to her parents—or perhaps they were her foster parents, I'm not sure—but I don't know how to find them."

"Condolences? What—like someone offed her?"

Rita raised an eyebrow. Now that, she thought, was interesting. Rita hadn't said anything about murder.

"Well, yes, actually...but why would you assume that?"

"I dunno. She just seemed like the type who wouldn't just die of angina or old age or something. There was always drama about her, and when there wasn't, she created it. At first, it made her kinda interesting, I guess. But after a while, it got old. And she was kinda uppity, you know? Like after a while, I kinda felt like the only reason she looked me up was to feel better about herself. And then she had that snooty French husband."

"He was Canadian, actually."

"Well, he *spoke* French." Suze rolled her eyes. "But I guess that must have ended in some kinda drama too because a couple of months ago there was an engagement announcement for her in the paper. Only she had a different name now."

"Greta Giroux?"

"Yeah." She snapped her fingers. "Like I said, French and snooty. I wouldn't have noticed it, but my old friend Katie called me up—she's a dentist now, but not half so snooty as Peggy—and told me to buy a paper, said Peggy was in it. And sure enough, I go to the wedding section and there she is, looking pretty much like she did in high school, but a little more gym bunny like and with blonder, straighter hair—none of that eighties poof, you know?—and straighter teeth. Maybe that French guy got her braces or something. The guy she was marrying was kinda old, though."

"Not old," Rita said primly. "Sixty."

"Yeah, like I said, kinda old." She shook her head. "Seems like that wedding was some kind of curse, doesn't it?"

Rita frowned. "What do you mean?"

"Well, I mean, she was supposed to get married and she was killed. But before that, there was an accident that I think was somehow related. A local guy who ran his truck off the road going a hundred and twenty miles an hour, straight into a tree. The cops said it was an accident, but I don't buy it."

Rita almost stopped breathing. "You think it was murder?"

195

"Murder? No—more like suicide. See, I recognized his picture in the paper. That was Peggy's old stalker—or the guy she claimed was her stalker. And when he died, he was clutching her engagement announcement in his hand." She pointed her tattoo removal laser—mercifully, still turned off—at Rita. "Now that last bit about him clutching the engagement announcement wasn't in the paper, but it's the worst-kept secret in town."

"How long ago was this?"

"Five, maybe six months ago. You could probably Google it. His name was Charles Wright, although he went by Chuck." She slid open a drawer and pulled out a yellow scrap of newsprint. "But I saved Peggy's engagement announcement. I dunno why—I guess out of some weird sense of loyalty because we used to be friends and it seems like I should care."

She handed it to Rita, and Rita scurried over to a chair in the corner, while Suze made Calvino lean back. "This won't hurt a bit," Suze said and then guffawed.

Rita tried to ignore Calvino's yelps, and the smell of burning flesh, as her eyes darted over the announcement.

Margaret (Peggy) Giroux née Wisniewski recently became engaged to Orlando Rinaldi, owner of the Rinaldi Winery in Morris County, New York. Ms. Wisniewski is a 1988 graduate of North Binghampton High School, where she was head cheerleader, senior class president, and Prom Queen. After graduation, she pursued a degree in business administration from SUNY Binghampton before transferring to SUNY Stony Brook in her junior year. Ms. Wisniewski had a successful career in sales and marketing before relocating to Morris County in 2016, where she met Mr. Rinaldi when she

experienced car trouble on the way up Passamaquody
Mountain and he rendered roadside assistance. She now is
assistant manager of the winery.

Ms. Wisniewski and Mr. Rinaldi will celebrate their
wedding on March 31st in an intimate ceremony at the
Rinaldi Winery, followed by dinner and dancing.

The announcement was accompanied by a dazzlingly
beautiful photo of Greta. Orlando was not in the
picture.

It wasn't much to go on, Rita thought, and in any
case, she couldn't see the connection to Greta's murder.
She got up, crossed the room, and handed it back to
Suze, who had just finished removing the tattoo from
Calvino. Calvino was holding an ice pack on his arm
and clutching it like it was on fire.

"Oh, no," said Suze, pressing it back into Rita's
hand. "You keep it."

Rita folded it and slid it in her purse. "So what was
this Charles like?"

"Chuck?" Suze just shook her head. "Goofy. A real
geek. While everyone else was moonlighting as a
bartender, he was trying to start a business as a Thomas
Jefferson impersonator, going around to local schools,
that kind of thing. I don't think it ever caught on,
although I guess he kinda looked like Jefferson. He
mighta been a little touched in the head, too, you know?
I mean, he wasn't dumb, but he just didn't understand
what people were really saying. He was super literal,
never got it when someone tried to give him the brush-
off."

"Like Greta—Peggy—you mean."

"Yeah, like Peggy."

"Did Chuck seem dangerous to you?"

"Not at all. I don't think he ever harmed Peggy, or even threatened her. I was her roommate at SUNY-Binghampton, see. He was always dropping by, leaving roses and little love notes, that kind of stuff. Oh, and lots of chocolate—I mostly ate that, since Peggy was worried about her figure. So for me, Peggy having a stalker wasn't all bad. And I don't even think it was bad for Peggy, either."

"Meaning?"

"It got her a lot of attention, a lot of sympathy, plus it made her seem like she was so hot guys were literally going crazy over her. Which got her even more male attention. Then it actually seemed to die down a bit, but Greta claimed he was crazier than ever, lurking in the bushes outside of classes, following her in his car, that kind of thing. She just said he wasn't coming around our room so much any more, maybe because I was there and he figured I'd keep him away from her. So that's when she hatched the plan to kill herself."

Rita just stared at Suze, who suddenly laughed.

"Not really," Suze said. "But she staged her own death so he'd leave her alone and, let me tell you, it was pretty impressive. That was Peggy—she never did anything halfway."

Chapter Twenty-Eight

Rita got Calvino some extra ice for his arm, a donut, and a lukewarm espresso (no hot beverages after dental work!) and plunked him down on a park bench while she paid a visit to the *Binghampton Sentinel*. By working some of her "we-reporters-are-all-in-this-together" charm, she was soon able to obtain the name of the person who had submitted the engagement announcement: Ida Brennan.

She raced back to the park bench and discovered that Calvino was in the middle of swapping fishing stories with a leather-skinned, flinty-eyed fellow who looked like he could have inspired "The Old Man and the Sea." She decided to leave Calvino there while she went to pay a social call on Ida.

Luckily, Ida lived not far away, in a tiny, neat-as-a-pin red-brick ranch house at the end of a tree-lined cul-de-sac. Lace curtains hung in the windows, and Rita could hear the sound of a canned laugh track, very loud, as she knocked on the door.

When no one answered, she moved to the one window in which the curtain had been pulled back and made frantic hand motions at the white-haired woman in a floral housedress who sat perched on a plastic-covered floral sofa. There was a TV tray in front of her, with what looked like the remains of breakfast, a walker on her left side, and an orange ball of fur in her lap.

The woman finally looked up, startled, snatched her walker, and lumbered to the door. Every step looked as if it hurt, and Rita felt terribly guilty for making her get up.

But then, she reasoned, this was all in the service of solving Greta's murder.

The door creaked open, and a bulging eyeball, robin egg's blue, regarded her. "Yes?" said a quavering voice.

This time, Rita saw no need for pretense.

"Rita Calabrese," she said, pulling out her press pass. The old woman squinted at it, and Rita surmised that her eyesight was probably failing so much that she couldn't distinguish a press pass from a police badge. So much the better. "I'm investigating the death of Margaret Wisniewski Giroux, and I was hoping you could help me."

"What did you say? I'm hard of hearing."

Rita repeated it again, even louder. She felt as though the whole block could hear her.

When she had finished, the woman stumbled backwards and grabbed the doorknob for support. "Death, did you say?" A pale, veiny hand fluttered to her chest. "Why didn't anyone tell me? They should have told me. I'm—I'm the next of kin."

Now it was Rita's turn to be taken aback. "You're her...."

"Grandmother."

****

Ida invited Rita in, turned off the "I Love Lucy" reruns, and sent Rita to the kitchen to brew them a pot of tea and rustle up some biscuits. The biscuits had expired six months ago, suggesting that Ida rarely had visitors, but Rita bravely choked down a couple of biscuits and a cup of tea before pleading her figure.

Then Rita said softly, "I'm sorry to be the one to tell you the news. I assumed that you knew."

"Well better you than no one," was Ida's sharp retort. "I should have known something was wrong when I never got my wedding invitation. I knew she wouldn't forget me like that."

"Did she visit often?"

"Oh, yes, maybe every two months. She'd take me out to lunch, take me to get my hair done, take me on long drives in the country. She was such a sweet girl. Had my chin too, you know, I don't care what anyone says."

She said this last statement with surprisingly ferocity. Rita squinted over her glasses at the woman's profile. She couldn't really see any resemblance, but that did not surprise her. Faces changed so much with age.

"So were you her paternal or maternal grandmother?" Rita asked.

"Paternal. She was my son Sean's child." Ida's lips were set in thin, determined line, as if daring Rita to contradict her.

"I guess Wisniewski must have been her stepfather, is that it?"

"Yes."

Rita looked around the cramped living room. In practically every nook and cranny there was a photo of Greta. But in none of them was she a child.

"Do you have any childhood photos of Peggy?" Rita said.

Ida shook her head, and a snow-white tendril fell in her eyes. Pushing it back impatiently, she said, "I didn't know her as a child, see. We reconnected later. I had been looking for my granddaughter for a long time, had even hired a few researchers to go through the records, that kind of thing. My son Sean—well, he sowed his wild oats in his youth, had a lot of drug problems. It was terrible. I felt like an utter failure as a mother." She shook her head grimly. "There was nothing more I could do for him, but I thought that perhaps I could make it up as a grandmother. And I figured he had some kids out there somewhere, I just didn't know where."

"And so one of these researchers found her?"

"Well, as luck would have it, she found them, actually. She happened to stumble on something they put on the Internet. A miracle, I tell you—an absolute miracle."

"Did you ask for any proof?"

"Proof—what kind of proof would she have? Her mother didn't put any father on her birth certificate, and I don't blame her. She was the right age, had my chin, and knew plenty about Sean. Plus, we got along famously—we were as thick as thieves." Her eyes misted over. "But—you said someone killed her?"

"She was poisoned," Rita said. "Someone switched water hemlock for wild carrots in her ingredient basket during a cooking competition."

"What is the world coming to?" Ida brushed away a few tears with the hem of her housedress. "My Peggy—my poor, poor baby." She started to rock gently. "Trouble seemed to follow her wherever she went. First that stalker, then the *French* husband—and you know how the French are—and now this Orlando."

With surprising venom, she suddenly shook her finger at Rita and said, "Ten to one, he did it."

"Orlando?"

"It's always the husband," Ida said grimly, "or the fiancé in this case."

"But what would the motive be?"

"Jealousy," Ida sniffed. "My Peggy was never a cheater, but that never stopped the men in her life from being jealous. She turned heads wherever she went. Or maybe they just wanted to get their grubby little hands on her money."

"But Peggy wasn't wealthy, was she?"

"No—at least not yet. She would have been if I'd died, though. I left everything to her."

Rita tried to stop herself from looking around the tiny house to see where all this fabulous wealth could be hidden. Unless the house were perched on an untapped gold mine, however, she could not quite imagine how Ida's death would make Peggy a wealthy woman.

As if reading her mind, Ida suddenly said, "I inherited ten thousand dollars from my Uncle Patrick in the nineties and, since he'd always dreamed of sailing down the Amazon—although of course he'd never gone further than Jersey—I invested in a company by that name on a whim. I knew nothing about it, not a thing. Just thought Uncle Patrick would be smiling down on me, that it seemed appropriate somehow. And now it's worth—goodness—maybe a hundred times that."

Rita did the mind-boggling math in her head. "Well, that certainly would make Peggy wealthy someday, but if Orlando was after her money why kill her before she inherited it?"

Ida frowned. "Well maybe he intended for me to die first."

"Was there an attempt on your life recently?"

"Well, no, but I have been getting some strange phone calls, you know, heavy breathing, hang-ups, that kind of thing."

Rita thought that sounded more like the handiwork of bored teens than a prelude to murder.

Ida leaned forward, fiddled with her dentures in the cup on the TV tray, then busied herself with tracing the patterns on her housedress. "There was a letter, too. All lies, vicious lies. But maybe that was a murder attempt. Maybe there were anthrax spores in the letter, or there was poison on the envelope flap. But I burned it—foiled their attempt."

"And what were these, er, lies, in the letter?"

"Oh"—Ida's eyes blazed—"wild rumors that Peggy wasn't really my grandchild and was just taking advantage of me. Probably someone in league with my greedy niece Irene, who never cared a fig for me until her mother told her I had invested in Amazon. Oh, how she hated Peggy! She never missed a chance to take a swipe at her. She even marched in here one day and insisted Peggy and I swab the inside of our cheeks so we could do some kind of genetic test. The nerve!"

"Where is this letter now?"

"Gone." Ida crossed her frail, withered arms across her chest defiantly. "I burned it."

Chapter Twenty-Nine

In the time Rita had been gone, Calvino had gone from stretching the truth to fabricating it out of whole cloth.

"One time," he was saying, "I took Bruce Springsteen out fishing for marlins. Now normally you can use mackerel or tuna for bait, 'cuz that's what marlins usually eat, but Bruce had an idea. He thought if we used a whole turkey as bait, we might be able to attract an even bigger fish. Because who doesn't like turkey? And sure enough, we caught an eighteen-foot-long marlin but then—"

Rita came up behind Calvino and clapped a hand on his shoulder. "Sorry to interrupt," she said, "but Bruce called and said it's urgent."

She hustled him back to the car.

"Happy now, Rita?" he asked as he got into the passenger seat and slammed the door. "I'm drooling like a ninety-year-old man"—he pointed at his fat novocaine-swollen lip—"I have painful blisters on my arm, and you cut me off midway through my best fishing story."

"Actually, I am happy." Rita started the car and backed out of the parking space. "I have plenty of fodder for an article on Greta's background, although of course all the sources are going to have to be off the record.

And I feel like I got some important information about who killed Greta."

"Oh, yeah? So who did it?"

"I don't know."

"Whaddya mean you don't know? You just said you did."

"No—I said I had more information." Rita looked in the rearview mirror and patted down the wiry black hairs that had escaped her huge bushy ponytail. "I didn't say I knew exactly how it fits together—or what it means. But my conversation with Ida gave me a much fuller picture of who Greta was—or wasn't. Not that Ida had the full picture. No, I'd say she had the wool pulled over her eyes—"

She was interrupted by her "*Va, Pensiero*" ringtone, which seemed to be coming from the backseat.

"Calvino, could you reach my phone?"

He reached around, wrestled with her purse, and finally extracted her phone, all while Rita attempted to concentrate on finding the on-ramp back onto the interstate. It was dusk already; at this rate, they'd be lucky to be back in Acorn Hollow by midnight.

His bushy gray eyebrows shot all the way up as he handed her the phone. "McFadden Correctional Center." He whistled. "Now who would you know there?"

"Oh, it's probably a wrong number. Give me that—yes, hello?"

There was a brief silence on the line, accompanied by a bit of static. In the background, rather muffled, she could hear shouts and the slamming of heavy metal doors.

And then, she heard, "Ma?"

"Vin?" Rita started to panic. "Why are you calling me from this number? What have you done?"

"Nothing, Ma, I swear. I mean, nothing that a million other kids don't do. But we tried to help out some girls and, well, the cops got the wrong idea."

"Help them out *how?*"

"Well there were these girls on the corner and they looked cold. I didn't know it could get this cold in South Carolina. And so me and Rocco offered them a ride and some food and then we got pulled over. And then it turned out the girls had some coke on them, but they claimed it was ours. And then there was some beer in the trunk, which we did buy, and technically my birthday isn't until next week...."

Rita groaned. "Vinnie, were these shivering, no doubt scantily clad girls hookers?"

"Well," he said miserably, "that's what the cops claimed. But me and Rocco didn't do nothing with them. I mean, they were kind of all over us, but nothing happened, I swear. I mean, I didn't know they were hookers. It's not like I asked them 'hey, what's your job? Like are you a hotel clerk, a lawyer, or a hooker?' before they hopped in the car."

"Vinnie," Rita sighed, "you're so naïve. What were they wearing?"

"I dunno. Some kind of skirt, real short, and one of those tops that's kind of like a big rubber band around their chest."

"A tube top?"

"Yeah—a tube top."

"Didn't that give you the idea they might be hookers?"

"Naw. I mean, Ma, all girls dress like that nowadays."

Rita frowned and thought of some of the get-ups she'd seen girls in last summer. Perhaps Vinnie had a point.

"Besides, Ma, you always taught us to see the best in people and help the less fortunate."

"I taught you that?"

"Sure, like how you're always dropping off food to neighbors out of work and leaving trays of lasagna for the family when somebody kicks the bucket." There was a loud man's voice in the background. "Ma—I gotta go. My two minutes are up. I have a bail hearing tomorrow at eleven."

"So—what? You want me to get you a lawyer? Post bail? You want me"—she paused dramatically—"*to meddle?*"

"Oh, you don't meddle, Ma. You just always fix things. You're a fixer, you know? Anyway, love ya, gotta go."

The line went dead.

"Trouble in paradise?" Calvino asked. "It's not all fun in the sun?"

"Yes, you could say that. See any cops?"

"No. Why?"

"Because I'm doing a U-turn and we're turning around. Next stop: South Carolina."

She slammed on the brakes, swerved onto the grassy median, and after a huge squeal of the brakes and a dramatic thunk, they were on the other side of the highway, accelerating back up to seventy.

Calvino was clutching his door handle and swearing in Italian under his breath. "Does Sal know you have this wild side?"

"Why do you think he married me?" Rita laughed. "Now we've got thirteen hours to put our heads together and figure out how to get Vinnie out of this pickle. I was thinking—"

Her phone rang again.

"Oh, dear, I hope it's not Gina saying 'I told you so.'" She fumbled with the phone and answered it without looking at the caller ID. "Hello? Oh—Concetta."

Calvino suddenly sat up very straight and stared at her. "Concetta? Why is she calling? What is she saying?"

Rita put her hand over the phone and glared at him. "Shhh. Oh—no, not you, Concetta. No, I'm just in a coffeeshop and I'm sitting next to this real loud-mouth. Oh, yes, it is a little late for coffee, but it's a poetry night. But don't worry—I'd much rather talk to you."

"Oh, good, because I really need someone to talk to," Concetta said, bursting into a sob. "Rita, I—I—I...."

"You—what?"

For a moment, Concetta was just sobbing into the phone, seemingly unable to say a word. It was so loud that Rita had to move the phone away from her ear.

Calvino tried to wrest the phone away from Rita, but she fought back, swerving so much she nearly hit the Volkswagen in front of her.

"I love you, baby! *Ti amo*, Concetta!" Calvino shouted.

Rita covered the phone and hissed at him, "Do you want me to hit the car full of kids and the adorable Golden Retriever? Do you want to ruin everything with Concetta? *Stai' zitto zitto!*"

Back into the phone, she said, "Sorry about that background noise. That loud-mouth keeps shouting 'I love you, baby,' to everyone! Between you and me, Concetta, I think he's already a bit in his cups. Now, you were saying, *cara...?*"

"I have"—Concetta let out a sound halfway between a sigh and a sob—"a lump. There—you know?"

"What did the doctor say?"

"Lots of stuff I didn't really understand. I was so scared, you know? I just kinda tuned him out. But it must be bad because he wants to cut me up! I'm gonna have scars, Rita; I'm gonna be less than a woman and that's if I'm not six feet under...."

Rita shot a quick glance at the clock and decided she'd just have to risk a speeding ticket if she was going to be at Vinnie's bail hearing by eleven.

"I'll be there in three hours," Rita said. "In the meantime, do you have someone you can be with? Maybe your kids?"

Concetta just wailed louder. "Daniella's off in Florida with her family"—Concetta made it sound as if her daughter was the most thoughtless, worthless girl ever, as if Daniella should have known her mother was going to get a cancer diagnosis—"and Frankie's in the clink again."

Rita almost said, "Yeah, so's Vin," but she decided against it. She always liked to have Concetta and the other relatives envy her for her near-perfect children. Besides, it didn't seem fair to lump Frankie and Vinnie together. Vinnie's stay in jail would be short and was surely the result of an honest misunderstanding. Frankie, well—Frankie was one of those kids for which the phrase "he's a bad apple" was invented. Rita had lost count of how many times he'd been in jail.

"And my no-good caveman of a husband," Concetta wailed, "just up and left. And at a time like this!"

"I was under the impression," Rita said, "that *you* kicked *him* out, and that was before you got this news."

"Well—maybe I did. But he deserved it. It's like living with a caveman. If I told him I had cancer, he'd probably grunt and ask when dinner's gonna be ready."

Rita looked over at Calvino, whose brows were deeply furrowed in concern. "Mmmm, somehow I doubt it. He really loves you, Concetta, even if he doesn't always know how to show it."

Calvino was nodding vigorously, as if Concetta could see him, and his puppy dog eyes were wet with unshed tears.

"*Ciao*, Concetta," Rita said. "*Ci vediamo pronto.*"

She stabbed the off button.

"Well?" Calvino demanded.

"Here's the good news: we're going to make a little detour to Atlantic City, and you're going to reunite with your wife, who is primed and ready for a reconciliation if you play your cards right."

Calvino leaned forward and tapped his foot. He looked both excited and anxious. "And the bad news?"

Rita said matter-of-factly, "She has cancer."

"Cancer?" Calvino pounded the dashboard so hard that Rita was worried his fist would go right through. "How could that be? Concetta's a saint. She doesn't smoke, she doesn't drink too much—okay, maybe too much wine on Saturday nights, but that's it, I swear—she eats kale and arugula and all kinds of weird healthy veggies I can't stand, she walks around the mall three times a week with her friends, swinging those little weights in her tight yoga pants. And she looks good in those yoga pants, even at her age!"

"At her age!" Rita said severely. Concetta was ten years her junior. "She's very young."

Ignoring her, Calvino continued his tirade. "I should get cancer, Rita, I mean I deserve it—I smoke cigars, I drink, I've got a big paunch, other than pumping iron I don't really exercise, I eat lots of red meat—"

Rita sighed. "Life isn't fair, Calvino. You know that."

"She's going to die, Rita, and leave me all alone. I'll be a widow—"

"Widower."

"I'll wear black for the rest of my life! Or maybe I'll just die from a broken heart. What will I do?"

He was in so much anguish that Rita pulled onto the shoulder, unbuckled her seat belt, and leaned over and gave him a hug.

"This is what you're going to do, Calvino. You're going to take Concetta into your arms and tell her how much you love her and how much you want her to be self-actualized and how empty your life would be without her. And whatever she wants to do in her treatment or recovery, you will support. Without question. No ifs, ands, or buts.

She eased back on the highway and hit the gas. "And then you will live happily ever after and darken our door no more."

Chapter Thirty

Around ten o'clock, Rita pulled off the expressway, stopped at a supermarket so Calvino could pick up some roses, and then drove past the seedy, neon-lit casinos that lined the route to Calvino and Concetta's brick rambler.

Calvino was wringing his hands anxiously, and the wringing sped up the closer they got. "What will I say?" he moaned. "What if I say the wrong thing?"

"Just channel Darcy," Rita said, "*after* he undergoes his transformation. And remember, the sweetest words in the English language are 'I love you,' 'I was wrong,' and 'I'm sorry.' Although, of course, they sound even sweeter in Italian."

"Maybe for chicks," he said. "The sweetest words for men are 'yes, you can go fishing with your buddies,' 'I made lasagna and cannoli for dinner,' and 'I shaved down there, bought a new negligee, and I don't have a headache tonight.'"

Rita shook her head and sighed. "I'll try to remember that."

She pulled to a stop in front of Calvino and Concetta's house. A light was on in the living room.

"No time like the present," she said, reaching over and unlatching his seat belt. Calvino seemed glued to the seat. "*Va'! Dai, Calvino, dai! Sii corragioso!*"

Calvino obeyed meekly, trudging up the driveway as if his feet were encased in lead. He joined her on the steps, and Rita pressed the doorbell twice.

She heard footsteps and then the door swung open.

"Rita!" Concetta exclaimed, and then, in a choked voice that managed to sound surprised, angry, and hopeful all at the same time, added, "Calvino!"

Concetta looked truly awful. She was wearing ratty flannel pajamas and big fluffy slippers, and she had her hair pinned up with curlers, the gray roots showing. The inky entrails of dried rivers of mascara—she had undoubtedly been crying—streaked down her face.

"*Bella, bella* Concetta!" Calvino whispered, awestruck.

Rita smiled. Only a man in love would say that. She pushed him forward. "Calvino insisted on coming with me," she said. "He really wants to be with you in your hour of need. You should have heard all the nice things he said about you. He was so upset. Weren't you, Calvino?"

When he said nothing, she nudged him.

"Concetta," he said solemnly, his voice cracking, "*ti amo*. With all my heart and soul. And I wanna support you in everything. If you lose a boob, that's okay. You'll be like those hot Amazonian women in that movie."

Concetta self-consciously put a hand on her breast. Rita had a feeling that Concetta was definitely in the reconstruction camp.

"If you wanna get new boobs—big ones, small ones, whatever—that's okay by me. If you need a wig, that's okay. You could be a blonde or a redhead or whatever. It might be kinda hot, you know? Mix things up a little."

Rita coughed loudly.

"Or"—Calvino looked nervously at Rita, then back at Concetta—"when you're feeling better, if you wanna be a community organizer or reporter or astronaut or tattoo artist or sumptin', I support that too. 'Cuz you're real smart, Concetta. I don't wanna stand in the way, and I'm real proud of you."

He cleared his throat and thrust into her hands the bouquet of red roses. "I love you, Concetta, even if I don't always say that. I've always loved you, I always will love you, and I want to spend the rest of our lives together, however long or short that is. Oh, yeah"—he jammed his hands in his pockets and frowned, as if trying to remember something—"and I was wrong and I'm sorry."

That must have finally done the trick because Calvino and Concetta collapsed into each other's arms. Rita wiped a few tears from her eyes, crept back down the driveway without bothering to say good-bye, got back in her car, and checked the time. She was going to have to drive at least ten miles over the speed limit if she was to get to South Carolina in time.

Rita screeched into the courthouse parking lot at ten forty-seven, used her scary mom voice to get a terrified young deputy to look up which courtroom Vinnie would be in, and raced up the marble staircase as fast as her thick ankles would carry her. She collapsed into a bench in the front of the courtroom and then frantically twisted this way and that until she finally spotted Vinnie, clad in an orange jumpsuit, at the back. Rocco, similarly attired and just as glum, was beside him.

Rita wondered just how much of her secret slush fund she was going to have to tap to get both Vinnie and Rocco out. They were going to owe her—big time. She compiled a mental list of all the chores she would have them do to repay her. The garage needed a new paint job, the fence needed mending, and then of course perhaps she could importune them to make some of her secret deliveries of homecooked food to certain down-on-their-luck neighbors. Plus, she could get them to do some investigating for the *Morris County Gazette*. Her newfound status as a celebrity journalist put some of the townspeople on guard when she tried to ferret out the truth, but no one would suspect Vinnie and Rocco.

Rita frowned. Was that meddling?

No, she decided, because there was a loophole for work.

The bailiff called Vinnie to the front, then Rocco. Vinnie waved shyly at her; Rocco acknowledged her with a little nod. Bail for each was set at twenty-five hundred dollars; Rita quickly did the math in her head and estimated that, if a bail bond was ten percent of the amount, it was going to cost her at least five hundred dollars to purchase bail bonds for both of them.

"Well," Rita muttered, "that's going to put a dent in my slush fund."

They then were paraded past her and taken back to their cells. She went to the clerk of court's office to write a check.

"I wish my momma was so generous," the clerk said as Rita handed over the check. "And my friends' mommas! Why, Rocco ain't even your child."

"Yes," Rita sniffed, "but do my children appreciate me? No."

"That ain't right," the clerk said. "Not right at all. They should thank their lucky stars—and stay out of trouble until their trial. You got a good lawyer lined up for them?"

Frowning, Rita murmured, "Not yet."

Rita shuffled back to the main office, sat on a hard plastic chair, and waited for Vinnie and Rocco to be released. She tried to estimate just how much a lawyer for the two of them might cost—and whether her slush fund was big enough to cover it. If it wasn't, she'd have to ask Sal, a thought that she did not relish. If it were Gina in trouble, she was sure he'd spring into action to save his little *principesa*. But when it came to Vinnie, she was rather less confident.

And then there was the whole problem of finding a competent lawyer in South Carolina. She didn't know a soul in South Carolina. Or did she...?

She dived into her purse for her phone and hit the speed dial for Detective Benedetto at the Acorn Hollow Police Department.

"Rita! Have you solved Greta's murder yet? I sure am glad this one's out of my jurisdiction."

"Not yet. Actually, I'm in South Carolina bailing Vinnie and Rocco out of jail."

"For what?"

"A complete misunderstanding. Listen, wasn't there a policeman who moved to South Carolina to be closer to his aging parents and got on the force there?"

"Bill O'Reilly."

Detective Benedetto gave her all the particulars, and her memory had served her well. Captain O'Reilly was a member of the very same police department that had arrested Vinnie and Rocco.

"Well, then," she said, "here's what we need to do...."

And she proceeded to tell him her plan. Out of the corner of her eye, she could see Rocco and Vinnie being led through a corridor behind plate glass.

"Detective?" she said. "I'm really sorry, but I've got to go. They're about to be released. *Mille grazie per tutto.*"

She was just about to click off when he said, "Wait a minute, Rita. There's something I wanted to tell you. I don't know if it helps or not, but the lab tests came back. You know, on the paper towels soaked with the wine that Julia Simms spilled after collapsing at the Carnevale ball?"

"Yes?"

Rita held her breath in anticipation. Rocco and Vinnie were coming towards her, so she held up a hand asking them to wait.

"Oleander," Detective Benedetto said. "She was poisoned with white oleander."

Thanking him profusely, she hung up. Then she gave each boy two *bacci* on their cheeks. "*Non ti preocupare,*" she told them. "Detective Benedetto's going to take care of everything. I expect the charges will be dropped before we even reach the state line."

"Huh?"

Rocco and Vinnie looked confused.

"You said I was a fixer, didn't you, Vin? So I fixed it." Rita shrugged and smiled modestly. "Of course, you will both be working off the bail bond money I spent on you, and you will both be on your absolute best behavior from now on. I'm not bailing you out twice."

She sandwiched herself between them and took them each by the elbow. They walked out into the blinding South Carolina sunshine. The air was balmy and smelled of the ocean. Rita sighed. It was a shame to have to leave this glorious weather for the much more temperamental springtime of Acorn Hollow.

But there was no time to spare.

Vinnie slid into the passenger seat, and Rocco curled up in the backseat.

"I'll just be a moment, boys," Rita said.

She stood in the parking lot, pulled out her phone, and dialed Sheriff D'Onofrio's number. "Sheriff," she said without waiting for him to launch into one of his lectures about not interfering in a police investigation, "I know who murdered Greta."

"What? Who?"

"Correction," she said, "I will know who murdered Greta after I make one phone call, send one email, and do a couple of Google searches."

"Huh?" Sheriff D'Onofrio seemed reduced to monosyllabic, incredulous expressions.

"Never you mind," she said. "Now, I want you to assemble all of the suspects for a briefing at the sheriff's office the day after tomorrow. And then I will reveal the truth."

Without waiting for his agreement, she rang off and called Orlando.

"Did Viola see you leave for the ball?" she asked.

"Yes, but—"

"And can you email me copies of all employment applications for your employees? You can black out the social security numbers."

"Sure, but—"

"Sorry, Orlando, but I've got to go. All will become clear in a couple of days."

She only had to wait a few minutes for the file with the employment applications. Then she scrolled through them, selected one, and sent it to Bianca. Then she conducted two quick Google searches. "I hope," she said to herself as she eased back into the driver's seat, "that the sheriff at least sends me a *cassata* as a gesture of his appreciation."

Chapter Thirty-One

Sheriff D'Onofrio paced the front of the conference room, while one of his deputies stood in the back. At Rita's insistence, the large conference room table had been wheeled out of the room and the chairs had been arranged in four rows of three. The only other furniture in the room was a small square table, on which sat four manila envelopes. Inside were several pieces of evidence—evidence that the sheriff's office had obtained at Rita's insistence. Sheriff D'Onofrio had ensured that the proper chain of custody had been followed, and that the evidence was correctly catalogued—but he did all this without knowing why most of it was significant. Rita had refused to say anything more except that, by the end of the day, he would be able to declare the case closed.

Rita greeted each guest warmly and ushered each one to his or her assigned seat.

"Front row seats," Teri tittered nervously as she and her two close friends, Aria and Diana, were seated in the front row. Today, as if by mutual agreement, all three had opted not to wear their pins protesting the proposed winery expansion. Had they finally developed a modicum of class? Rita wondered. Or had they decided that, when summoned to police headquarters, it would be imprudent to advertise their motive for murder?

Aria flipped open her compact and touched up her lipstick, as if expecting a TV camera to emerge at any moment.

"Best seats in the house," she said with a shrug of her slim, bare shoulders. Despite the chill outside, she was wearing a white halter top, the better to show off her salon tan, and tight jeans. "And I'm sure Rita will put on quite a good show." She shot a smile at Rita. "Won't you, Rita? I've been dying to see the great sleuth of Acorn Hollow in action."

It might have been Rita's imagination, but she detected a hint of sarcasm in Aria's voice.

"I do not intend," Rita said with an icy smile, "to disappoint. Although whoever ends up getting arrested may not think this was such a 'good show.'"

Aria laughed. "Oh, well, certainly I've got nothing to worry about. I'm a vegan—practically a Jain. I couldn't kill a fly. Everybody knows that. And I'd hardly have stooped to murder to stop the winery expansion; I already had the county board eating out of my hand, and I'm sure I would have won at the hearing."

Rita rather doubted that, as she thought Greta's charm and wiles far exceeded Aria's, but she was willing to let Aria think that for that moment. She shifted her attention to Teri, who was sinking lower into her seat and watching Sheriff D'Onofrio's every move. Clearly, she did not share her friend's confidence.

On Aria's other side, Diana seemed unperturbed. Taking a cue from Aria, she fluffed up her hair and took a nail file from her purse.

The winery crew—Orlando, Bianca, Viola, and Jack—arrived next. "You three," Rita said, "should sit in the second row. Viola on the left, Orlando in the middle, and Bianca on the right. Jack must go in the third row, on the right."

Orlando, Bianca, and Jack dutifully took their seats, but Viola took her time about it. When she finally sat down, she perched on the edge of her seat. Her beady dark eyes roamed around the room, noting exactly who was in each seat.

"Ah," Viola finally remarked, "I'm in Greta's place."

Teri spun around in her chair and seemed to shiver. "What do you mean?"

"Well, isn't it obvious?" Viola said. "The night Greta was murdered, we were in the room where Rinaldis' gives cooking classes. There were twelve cooking stations, eleven of which were occupied. Teri, Aria, and Diana were in the first row"—she pointed at each of them in turn—"and in the second row were Greta" -she pointed at herself—"Orlando, and Bianca. And in the third row were Rita and Rose"—she indicated two empty chairs— "and Jack."

Bianca frowned and knitted her dark eyebrows together. Jack nodded as if he'd already worked that out, and Orlando nodded slowly, as if the pieces of the puzzle were just fitting together.

Rita peered over her glasses at Viola. "You're certainly in Greta's *seat*," she said, "but I don't think anyone can take Greta's *place*."

Their little exchange seemed to be lost on everyone else, but Viola's pursed lips told Rita she fully understood her meaning—and didn't like it one bit.

Rose rushed in next, with McKenzie and Luca right behind her. Now that Viola had worked out the schema, she apparently could not help herself from taking charge, directing them as if they were pieces on a chessboard. "Rose," Viola said, "you're here on the left, the chair in between must stay empty—that's Rita's chair—and Jack, you're on the right. McKenzie, you go in the last row on the left and Luca, you sit beside her." Her beady eyes turned back to Rita. "And who's the mystery guest in the last chair? Or does that stay empty?"

As if on cue, Orlando's ex-wife appeared in the doorway just then. "Ah—Marie." Rita clapped her hands. "If you'd be so good as to sit in the last chair there. Perfect." She beamed at all assembled as a teacher beams at her obedient pupils. "I asked Marie to join us because, well, anything concerning the winery—of which she is still part-owner—certainly concerns Marie. Financially, of course, but also personally as Orlando's ex-wife, Bianca's mother, and Teri's aunt."

"But," Marie objected, "Teri doesn't work at the winery."

"No," Rita agreed amicably, "but given that her land abuts the winery, she would be very much affected by the expansion—the expansion that Greta was the driving force behind."

Marie scowled. "Whoever offed Greta did us all a world of good, but it wasn't Teri."

Orlando turned beet-red, balled up his fists, and turned around to confront his ex, but Rita silenced him by holding up her hand.

"Oh, no?" she said innocently. "And how would you know, Marie? You weren't there the night that Greta was murdered. But everyone else who was actually there is assembled here—except, of course, Calvino, but since he had no prior interaction with Greta and therefore could not possibly have a motive, and his wife was just diagnosed with cancer, the sheriff agreed to excuse him from this little exercise. Isn't that right, Sheriff?"

Sherriff D'Onofrio furrowed his brow and nodded with a sigh. He clearly was not pleased about Rita running the show, although he had little choice. "That's right," he said.

The sheriff cleared his throat. "Now, I know this is a little unusual, asking you to come down here and all. And having Rita run the briefing. But I thought that it might be good to get a fresh perspective on the case." He nodded at her. "So, Rita, please proceed."

"Now," Rita continued, "the sheriff tells me that the medical examiner's report confirms what I suspected, that Greta died as a result of ingesting water hemlock, a plant that Viola specifically pointed out to us all as poisonous. Greta was nothing if not meticulous, so I have no doubt that she would have heeded Viola's warning."

"I do," Bianca said sullenly, kicking at the floor. She looked up and locked eyes with Rita. "She was so busy making googly eyes at my dad, she might not have paid any attention."

"Bianca!" Orlando's voice was uncharacteristically sharp. Normally, he was a very indulgent father. "Rita, I can assure you that she and I both listened to Viola's warning."

Rita picked up one manila envelope and slid out two enlarged photographs, brandishing them at those assembled as though she were a star prosecutor and they the awestruck jury.

The photos had been taken just a few seconds apart and showed Greta looking right at Viola, not touching Orlando, as Viola pointed at the telltale mottled stem of the water hemlock.

"So someone swapped out the water hemlock for her wild carrots," Jack said, "during the competition."

He had the eager look of a normally dim-witted student who had finally been coaxed into giving the right answer and now wanted a pat on the head.

"That was my theory," Rita admitted.

Aria said, "She was making wild carrot soup. I remember overhearing that photographer—Calvin, was it?—asking her. At least, she *thought* it was wild carrot soup."

"And Viola," Diana said accusingly, pointing her nail file in Viola's direction, "did keep urging us to taste as we went along, since the ingredients didn't taste quite like their store-bought counterparts."

Everyone swiveled to stare at Viola.

"So," Rita asked, "did anyone see Greta leave her cook station unattended?"

Orlando shook his head. "Other than leaving to grab ingredients from the pantry that one time, I think she was at her cook station the entire time."

"Does everyone agree?" Rita asked.

Eleven heads nodded in agreement.

Rita selected a second manila envelope and took out a thick stack of photographs. For dramatic effect, she held each one up in quick succession, then slapped them down on the table. "Now, these photographs show everyone crowded around in a mad dash to get ingredients from the pantry. Everyone here except Marie—who of course was not in attendance—and Viola, who of course was the judge, is in these photographs, all time-stamped, by the way. Now, Orlando and Bianca are only in the first few frames—"

"Because," Bianca said hotly, "we knew where everything is and so could get our ingredients right away."

Nodding reassuringly, Rita said, "Which makes perfect sense, as you say. And no one else disappeared from the frame for more than three seconds, which would hardly be enough time to run to Greta's station and back to the pantry. Nevertheless, for the moment, let's agree that the only people who could have tampered with Greta's ingredients while she was in the food pantry were Orlando, Bianca, and Viola."

"But Bianca never went near Greta's workstation," Orlando insisted.

Bianca then leapt to his defense. "And my dad didn't either. At least, not while she was in the pantry."

All eyes turned on Viola.

"She is an expert is poisons," Jack said.

"She had plenty of time to tamper with Greta's cook station," Teri said, "either while Greta was in the pantry—or during the competition. I mean, Viola was circulating constantly, offering tips and advice."

"Yeah," Rose said. "Viola is always so *helpful*"—she heaped scorn on the last word—"and she always hated Greta."

Orlando frowned. He seemed to be the only person surprised by Rose's remark.

Viola looked pale and frightened. She seemed to shrink before their hard, inquisitive looks. "I think," she said weakly, "I could use a bathroom break."

Chapter Thirty-Two

Rita winked at the deputy standing outside the ladies' room, slipped inside, and waited for Viola to emerge from a mint-green stall. There, in front of a chipped, graffitied mirror, Rita had one of the most interesting—and most gratifying—heart-to-hearts of her entire life. When she and Viola walked back into the conference room, Viola was looking slightly green, but Rita was feeling refreshed and rejuvenated.

"So," Marie huffed, "it was Viola, right? Can't you just hurry up and arrest her so we can all get on with our day?"

Rita demurred. "Patience, Marie. Patience. I could not have deduced that Viola was the murderer from the crime scene alone. If I could be sure that the water hemlock was substituted for the wild carrots at Greta's cook station, then the only possible suspects would be Orlando, Bianca, or Viola—or perhaps all three colluding together, providing each other with an alibi. But there would certainly not be enough evidence for an airtight case. So if that were all we had to go on, we'd be at a dead end. "

"But"—all eyes were on her now—"if we allow for the possibility that the water hemlock was put in Greta's basket before her arrival at the winery—say, during the commotion when Bianca fell through the ice—then anyone *except* Bianca could have made the substitution, changing the case entirely."

"So," Marie said from the back of the room, "we're back to anyone could have done it. Except me, of course."

"That would be true if it were not for the fact that there is an additional crime scene to consider—the poisoning of Julia Simms at the Carnevale ball." Rita turned towards the hallway. "Julia, could you come in now, please?"

There was a ripple of excitement as Julia Simms walked into the room. As instructed, she was wearing the gown that she had borrowed from Greta and worn to the Carnevale ball. Her flaxen hair was arranged in a stunning up-do, and her watch had once more been removed. A bejeweled velvet mask covered her face, leaving only her mouth and chin exposed.

"A poisoning," Rita said, raising her voice to be heard over the murmuring, "that, I believe, was a case of mistaken identity. Because, as you can see, Julia Simms could easily be mistaken for Greta Giroux in this outfit, particularly in the lower light of St. Vincent's basement. So, then, it becomes a matter of determining who was at St. Vincent's that night, who was definitely not at St. Vincent's, and who could have been at St. Vincent's. So who was definitely in attendance? Rose, myself, Orlando, Bianca, McKenzie, Luca, and Marie. Do any of you deny it? No? Good. And who was definitely not there? Well, only Aria and Diana seem to have good alibis, as they were at a yoga retreat in the Berkshires, although it is just possible they could have snuck out, committed a murder, and driven back. But, I think that's unlikely. That leaves Teri, Jack, and Viola as question marks.

"I was at home," Jack said. "It was my day off."

"I was at home, too," Viola insisted, her spine ramrod-straight, her eyes flashing. She was still smarting from Marie's accusation. "I had just finished my shift and was exhausted."

"And I had the flu," Teri said meekly. Her dark eyes were wide, and she had the look of a scared, cornered rabbit.

From the back of the room, Marie said, "I can vouch for my niece. I called her twice from the ball to check on her. She was very ill."

Rita waved her hand dismissively. "So we have two alibis that can't be verified and a third that is only backed up by a beloved aunt who could have conspired with her niece to kill Greta."

Julia bit her lip and, since her mouth was just about the only part of her visible, the effect was magnified. "Marie," she said softly, "did bump Greta at the ball and cause her to spill her drink. Or at least someone did—and Greta was sure it was Marie."

"Yes—Teri and Marie certainly would have made a formidable team," Rita said. "But there are several problems with this theory. First, no one recalls Marie bumping Julia—whose drink was actually poisoned—and no one saw Marie put anything in Julia's drink. In fact, no one saw anyone tamper with Julia's drink, which suggests that poison was added to her cup before it was handed to her. Now, Julia, tell us who handed you the cup?"

"Orlando." Julia glanced at Orlando briefly, blushed, and then looked at the floor. "At least, I thought it was Orlando because he was wearing that costume, the uh...."

"*Medio delle peste*," Rita supplied. "But Julia, did you ever hear Orlando speak?"

"No."

"No—that is very significant. So, it might not have been Orlando—especially when you consider that I noticed there were two people that night wearing a *medico delle peste* costume. Now, Julia, could the person who brought you the drink have been Marie?"

"No, I don't think so, because, uh...."

Rita sensed Julia's hesitation. Even during a murder investigation, sweet, gentle Julia was reluctant to hurt anyone's feelings.

Rita had no such compunctions, particularly for someone as loathsome as Marie. "What Julia is trying to say is that the person was taller and slimmer than Marie."

Ever since her divorce, Marie had expanded to near Marion-sized proportions.

Rita went on. "So that eliminates Marie, although not, perhaps, her possible accomplice, Teri, who is slim and could have been wearing lifts in her shoes. The same goes for Viola, Bianca, and McKenzie, and Jack and Luca could have been mistaken for Orlando as well."

Teri said, "But you said it couldn't have been me, right?"

Rita nodded. "I knew it couldn't be—or at least was extremely unlikely to be—Teri, or Luca or McKenzie for that matter, because of the poison used. The sheriff here was kind enough to accede to my request to share the results of the lab tests done on Julia's wine." She selected a third manila envelope, took out a thin sheet of paper, and slowly unfolded it. "Oleander," she said. "White oleander."

Viola gasped and turned deathly pale. Everyone turned to stare at her once more.

"Yes, Viola," Rita said, "and the source was no doubt the water from the vases filled with the white oleander that graced the tables of Rinaldi Winery the day of the Carnevale ball. White oleander that you ordered, overriding Greta's choice of roses."

"Viola," Orlando wailed, "what have you done?"

Viola's eyes darted around the room, searching for a sympathetic face but finding none.

"That was my thought, too," Rita said. " 'Viola, what have you done?' But then I realized that Viola would not have made the murderer's biggest mistake."

Rita paused. She could see everyone trying to work out just what this mistake might have been.

"You see," she said, "Julia was wearing a mask, of course, just like today, so the only clues as to her identity were her height and build, very similar to Greta's; her blonde hair, a shade darker that Greta's perhaps, but that would have been hard to distinguish in the dim light of St. Vincent's basement; and of course her dress—which she had borrowed from Greta, and which was the dress Greta initially had planned to wear. And then this"—Rita brought Julia's wrist up to her face and turned it outwards for all to see—"a tiny butterfly tattoo that is an exact match to one Greta had in the exact same place. They got it together in high school. And right before the person she thought was Orlando offered her a drink, Julia raised her arm to re-arrange her hair"— Rita demonstrated, arranging Julia's limbs as if she were a mannequin—"thus exposing the tattoo. The murderer sees the tattoo, the blonde hair, maybe even the dress he or she expects Greta to be wearing and thinks 'aha— that's definitely Greta.' Then the person hands Julia the poisoned wineglass."

"But Viola," she explained to mostly blank stares, "would not have made this mistake. Why? Because she'd seen Orlando, Bianca, and Greta leave for the ball as she was finishing up her shift. She knew that Greta was wearing a burgundy ball gown. So there's no way she would have confused Julia for Greta. The same goes for Orlando, of course, and Bianca. So, then I asked myself: who is the one person who was at or could have been at the ball, had access to the oleander water at the winery and knew it was poisonous, and believed Greta would be wearing an emerald green gown?"

The room was very still.

"The answer," she said, "is Jack."

Chapter Thirty-Three

"Jack?" the room said in unison over the sharp click of handcuffs.

"It seems unlikely, I know," Rita said. "But only if you assume that he is what he makes himself out to be—a would-be teacher who is working at the winery to earn a little cash before going back to school. But what if Jack had a very specific reason for getting a job at the Rinaldi Winery, a reason rooted in the last time his path and Greta's crossed? What if he came here with murder already in his heart? What if he came here under an assumed name?

"If I'd been listening—really, truly listening—to my beautiful, brilliant daughter Gina, I would have realized that Jack was more than met the eye. First, Gina happened to mention that he'd been an Outward Bound counselor and a birder which meant, although I failed to realize it at the time, that he was probably much more familiar with poisonous plants than he let on.

"Then there was the fact that there was only one mention of him on the Internet, when he won a swim meet in high school. At a time when young people are posting what they put on their toast for breakfast—which is a silly thing to boast about, as they should be eating delicious biscotti—that's unusual to say the least. And when I finally Googled him, I saw that the picture of Jack MacDougall with a swim cap and goggles could have been almost any athletic young man.

"And then, of course, there was the additional information I dug up on Greta in Binghampton. Greta, it turned out, had a stalker—or at least thought she had a stalker, or wanted everyone else to think she had a stalker. In any case, there was a young man desperately infatuated with her when she was in college. She felt so threatened—or so in need of attention—that she faked her own death, letting her old junker of a car roll over a cliff in view of him, putting her obituary in the paper, changing her name, and having a friend reach out to him to deliver the news personally. Then recently, this same man commits suicide—with her engagement announcement from the Binghampton paper beside him. Why? Probably because this was the first time he realized he'd been duped—and that she'd been alive this whole time. And, this knowledge—this betrayal—drove him to suicide.

"Now, I would not have connected the suicide to Jack here—let's just call him Jack for the moment—were it not for two interesting coincidences. First, someone who knew the suicide victim made an offhand remark that he'd been a Thomas Jefferson impersonator, which made me suspect he was a redhead, like our Jack here. And second of all, because, at Greta's funeral, I overheard Jack tell the story of how Greta and Orlando met, but he got it wrong. I didn't realize it at the time, of course. But when I asked Orlando how they he and Greta met, I discovered they met line dancing. So why did Jack say Orlando and Greta met when Greta's car broke down on Passamaquody Mountain and he gave her assistance? Because"—she reached for the fourth manila envelope and pulled out a newspaper clipping—"he hadn't heard the story from Greta or Orlando directly. He'd gotten the story from this announcement in the Binghampton paper—the same announcement that was found next to the suicide victim. An announcement that got the story of how they met wrong.

"And then, the final clue—the handwriting on the note that lured Bianca out onto the frozen pond that day, creating the perfect opportunity to put the water hemlock in Greta's basket. It matched the handwriting in Jack's application for employment."

"So Jack is the suicide victim's son?" Aria asked.

"Well, the *real* Jack MacDougall is the suicide victim's nephew. He really did win a swim meet, but sadly, shortly afterwards, he developed schizophrenia and is now in an institution—which explains the lack of an Internet presence—and why he never reported his identity stolen when Archibald Wright started using it. But, yes, Archibald"—she clapped a hand on his shoulder, and he grimaced—"is the suicide victim's son."

"It wasn't suicide!" Archibald shouted. "*She* killed him. She let him believe that she had died, so that he spent the rest of his life pining over this mythical perfect woman who died tragically young. My mother felt like a poor consolation prize their entire married life. And then he saw that stupid announcement in the paper and killed himself. And two months later she was gone, too."

Tears welled up in Rita's eyes. Archibald has no siblings; he was all alone in the world now. "So she committed suicide, too?"

"No—she died of a broken heart. She had stage three cancer, had been fighting it for years. It would go into remission and then come back. But my mother always fought on. She was the bravest, strongest woman I knew. And then, after he died, she told me she had no reason to live. It wasn't just that he died, but that this woman— this awful, self-centered woman—had such a strong grip on him that, decades after they'd last seen each other, she could drive him to suicide. As if my mother's love and fidelity meant nothing to him."

"But," Rita said, "you were still there for her."

Archibald laughed bitterly. "I guess I wasn't enough."

Rita suddenly felt very world-weary. What a tragedy. Archibald loved his mother enough to commit murder for her—yet his love was not enough for her. Archibald's mother's love for her husband was so great that her life literally depended on his—yet this was not enough for him. And Greta had loved no one so much as herself.

Rita's eyes filled with tears. She wanted to run home and tell her family how much she loved them—that they were all enough for her. She even had a sudden, strange urge to call Calvino and Concetta and invite them for Easter dinner.

The deputies forced Archibald to his feet.

"Hey, Rita," Archibald said.

Rita wiped away a tear. "Yes?"

"Please apologize to Gina on my behalf. I guess I won't be able to go birding with her on Saturday."

Rita groaned. She had no idea how to break the news to Gina. Her daughter had the absolute worst luck when it came to men. The only consolation this time was that at least Rita hadn't encouraged the match, but that was cold comfort.

When he was led out of the room and down the corridor, Aria began to snicker. "Archibald?" she said. "What a horrible name!"

Chapter Thirty-Four

Rita was the last to leave the room. She shook hands with Sheriff D'Onofrio, who had the good grace to at least thank her for her efforts. "Although next time," he said, "I'll think we'll handle it ourselves."

Rita laughed. "I think we both know that's not true."

Leaving him speechless, she hurried out to the parking lot. Catching a glimpse of Orlando's gold Lexus turning onto the main road, Rita slammed the door and hit the accelerator. She was going to do whatever it took—yes, even if that meant *meddle*—to keep Greta from claiming one more life.

She followed him down dappled country lanes, past white picket fences, tidy cottages, and rolling hills. The trees were just beginning to bud; the roadside was lined with wildflowers.

It was Spring at last, she thought, and nearly Easter. It was—or should be—a time of new beginnings, of rebirth. She hoped Orlando saw it that way as well, although the knot in her stomach told her otherwise.

Her phone rang.

"Rita?" It was her sister. "I've finally uncovered something about Viola. Something big. So as I was leaving your little briefing—good job catching the murderer, by the way, I did not see that coming—I was talking to—"

"Don't worry about it, Rose. Your problem's solved."

"It is?"

"You remember how Viola and I disappeared to the ladies' room for a bit? Well, I convinced her that in exchange for keeping my mouth shut, she would stop blackmailing everyone and would return the money to all of her victims."

"But what dirt did you have on her?"

"*Niente*," Rita said. "*Assolumente niente*. I finally realized the one point of leverage we really have—and that's that, deep down, she's a woman in love. A woman with a senseless, unrequited love and, as badly as she may have treated Orlando out of some misplaced rage and jealousy, the one thing she cannot abide is that he will think less of her. And if I were to tell him that she was blackmailing him and his beloved Greta, well, that would certainly sour their relationship."

"And that was it?"

"That was it. Love conquers all." Although not, she added to herself, always in a good way.

"But," Rose said, "don't you want to know—?"

"No, actually," Rita said. "I don't want to hear a single thing more that will further lower my opinion of the human condition." She braked hard, suddenly. "*Accidenti!*"

"*Che c'e?*" Rose asked.

"Oh, I missed a turn. I'm tailing him, you see."

"Who?"

"*Mi dispiace*, sis, but I've got to go call Calvino."

243

"Calvino!"

Rita rang off over Rose's mutterings of wonder. She pulled a sharp U-turn and turned down the road Orlando had taken. She could just make out his car as a dot on the horizon. She accelerated sharply, and the dot grew slightly larger.

She dialed Calvino's number. "How's my husband's favorite cousin?" she said warmly. "And my favorite cousin-in-law?"

"Aw, Rita, I'm doing great, thanks to you. I mean, I'm bummed about Concetta's cancer, of course, but I talked to the doc, and it sounds like they're just gonna be able to pop that sucker right out. The tumor, that is. And then she's gonna get herself a new pair of—"

Rita coughed loudly into the phone.

"Well, ya know what I mean," he said apologetically. "They're gonna be bigger and better than ever. And then I'm gonna take her on a trip to...."

"Florida?"

"Nope. Italy! Can ya believe it?"

Actually, she couldn't. For the first time in her life, she was jealous of Concetta. She wished Sal were taking her to Italy.

Without waiting for a response, Calvino plowed on. "I asked her where she wanted to go and she said Italy! So we're gonna go to southern Italy—look up some of the relatives, drink wine and eat seafood by the shore, see some old temples. We're even going to Pompeii. It's kinda like a metaphor, see? Out of ruin can come beauty. Like out of this big fight with Concetta and her cancer and all can come a new beginning for us."

Rita nearly dropped her phone. She would never have guessed that Calvino even knew what a metaphor was, let alone that he could use it in such a poetic way.

"And I owe it all to you, Rita," he said. "Ya know, if this whole reporter thing, doesn't work out, maybe you could start like a camp, or a retreat or sumptin', for husbands who need to learn how to improve their relationships. Or maybe you should write an advice column, too. You could call it 'Ask a Dudette.'"

She was coming into Acorn Hollow now. Ahead of her, Orlando's car pulled into a driveway on the left and Bianca got out in front of her neat brick rambler.

Rita hung back and idled by a beautiful meadow carpeted with wildflowers. She smiled. "Oh, I don't know," she said. "I think Sal's got the advice market cornered in Morris County."

Orlando pulled out onto the main road again, and she eased back onto the road too.

"And it turns out," Sal said, "that Concetta doesn't want to be a community activist or astronaut or sumptin' like that. She just wants to do art. See, she was really arty in high school, but then I knocked her up so she didn't get to do nothing like that. But she wants to put a pottery wheel in our basement and start making pots."

"Oh—that's wonderful, Calvino! I want to be one of Concetta's first customers. I'd love a really unique planter for my front porch. And maybe Sal could sell some of her pots at the nursery."

"Yeah, that'd be swell, Rita. You're a real brick, ya know that?"

She followed Orlando as he turned down Viola's street. He let her out, and Rita watched her birdlike little frame and helmet of dyed black hair disappear through the gate. She walked with stiff, almost exaggerated dignity which concealed, Rita suspected, more than a little wounded pride. Viola's power was spent; Rita would make sure that she never returned to her old shenanigans. From now on her pastimes would be strictly limited to experimenting with Puerto Rican love potions and reading steamy romances.

And Rita suspected that would be as close as Viola ever got to romance, at least with Orlando. It didn't matter whether Marie or Greta were in or out of the picture; Orlando's feelings for Viola would never go beyond admiration and respect.

Viola closed the gate with a loud clang, and Orlando was off again. Rita hit the gas, too, her heart beating faster. Orlando was completely alone now. Just how alone did he feel? And how desperate?

Orlando made a few more turns. He was heading down towards the river.

Down to the cemetery.

"Calvino," Rita said quickly, "I'm so glad everything worked out for you and Concetta, but I really do have to go. I was wondering, though, if you and Concetta would like to come to our Easter dinner this Sunday."

"Really? You mean it?"

"*Certo!*" She surprised even herself with her enthusiasm.

"Then it's a deal," he said. "No one does Easter better than you, even Concetta—but don't tell her I said that. We'll bring the wine."

She threw her phone onto the passenger seat and pulled into the cemetery behind Orlando. The gravel crunched under her tires as she wended her way down the long, curving road. As she came over the rise by the old hickory tree that shaded her mother's grave, she spotted him. He was standing on Greta's grave. His back was to her; his shaved head shone bright in the sunlight. His head was bowed and his shoulders were shaking, as if he were crying.

And there was something glinting in his right hand.

She braked hard, sprang out of the car, and ran as fast as her thick ankles could carry her, half-tripping over tree roots and moss-eaten fallen tombstones. "Orlando!" she cried. "No! Orlando—don't do it!"

Her voice sounded strange in the wide-open expanse. It was high-pitched, shrill, carried by the wind like the howl of a banshee.

"Orlando! No—!"

In a moment, she would close the distance between them. He spun around suddenly and stared at her. His eyes were hollow, expressionless, but there was a deep furrow in his brow.

"How did you~?" he began, but his words were swallowed up by the wind.

"Give me the gun, Orlando," she begged him. "Just put it down and kick it over to me."

He looked down at his hand almost as if he had forgotten it was there, or as if its sinewy muscles belonged to some other person. Then he shook his head firmly as if jolted back to reality.

247

"It's no use, Rita." His face was streaked with tears, and they just kept coming. "What have I got to live for? I'm a screw-up, a total screw-up and a terrible judge of character. I married Marie against everyone's advice, and look how that turned out. Then I got engaged to Greta, whom apparently I never knew at all, and then managed to be stupid enough to hire and trust Jack, who turned out to be a murderer!"

Rita took a step closer to him. He didn't flinch or step back, so she figured that was a good sign.

"Bianca," she said softly. "That's who you have to live for. Your daughter loves you more than anything. She loved you far more than Marie ever did, or Greta. And if there's one reason not to kill yourself, that's it. Look how Jack's father's suicide turned him into a monster. It ruined Jack's life, his mother's life, and then it ruined Greta's life. Is that what you want for Bianca?"

"No."

She noticed that his grip on the gun loosened slightly.

"And as for the other women in your life," Rita said, "so you married a shrew the first time. That happens to a lot of men. And it wasn't all bad—you got Bianca out of it, and Marie did have a good head for business. She helped you make the winery what it is today."

He nodded ever so slightly.

"And as for Greta, I'm quite convinced that she did love you. She wasn't so much a gold-digger or an opportunist as a survivor. So she survived by telling people around her stories, by telling herself stories. Who's to say what was or wasn't true? There's always a gap between how we see ourselves and how others see ourselves; we all change our perception of the world to suit our own needs." Softly, she added, "Even me."

Rita went on. "Her friends in Binghampton told me that even when what she said wasn't strictly true, it had the essence of truth. She turned her sordid life—her father a burglar, her mother run off to California, raised by foster parents—into something much more beautiful and interesting, something much more worth living. In her world, her mother was an actress, her father was a cop, and her foster parents were a loving aunt and uncle. It gave her joy, it gave her purpose—and she transmitted that joy and purpose to others. You want to know why she was blackmailed?"

Orlando frowned. "An affair?"

"No—she had shaded the truth, just a bit, to invent a grandmother, and in the process brought incredible joy to an old woman who had been searching for her grandchildren for years."

"Ida wasn't actually her grandmother?"

Rita shook her head sadly.

Orlando eyed her suspiciously. "Is Ida rich?"

"Yes,"—Rita waved a hand dismissively—"but Greta couldn't possibly have known that. The old woman lives in as humble a house as you could imagine."

"But Greta deceived her."

"I rather think," Rita said, "that Greta may have deceived herself as well. But even if she didn't—even if she knew Ida wasn't her grandmother—her deception did Ida a world of good. What is a dream, after all, but a wonderful deception? Holding on to something too good to be true?" Rita's eyes misted over. "No one would ever fall in love if they never wanted to be deceived. We all know, deep down, that we'll wake up someday and realize our spouse is balding, snores like a freight train, and leaves dirty dishes in the sink."

Orlando actually laughed.

"And that's what Greta was—better than the real thing. She was better than a real granddaughter to Ida. She wasn't one of these ungrateful grandkids that send a birthday card and flowers once a year. She drove several hours every month or two to take her out and about. She took her on picnics and country drives; she took her to the hairdresser. She called her every Sunday. Greta sprinkled a bit of fairy dust into her life—and into yours, too."

He seemed to be mulling this over. "And what about Jack's father? Was he really stalking her?"

"I don't think we'll ever know." Rita sighed. "But I think it's entirely true that she became convinced he *was*—even as he was convinced he *wasn't*. One woman's stalker is another woman's ardent lover. What happened then, what happened now—it's all a tragedy."

She took a step closer. She was almost close enough now to reach out and grab his gun.

"Let's not compound that tragedy," Rita said, "with yet another one."

She was about to take the final step when she heard a faint whirring sound and a crunch of gravel behind her.

"Oh, for goodness sake," Rita heard, and she spun around to see the widow Schmalzgruben at the helm of her golf cart. As usual, she was clad in black, buttoned-up boots and a black long-sleeved dress. To ward off the chill, she had added a black cape; her accent of red was a ruby-encrusted choker.

"You young people are far too dramatic," the widow said in her rich, plummy voice, sounding exasperated.

Only the widow, Rita thought, could refer to sixty-year-old Orlando as young.

"Why," the widow continued, shaking a pale, veiny finger at him as though he were a naughty boy, "I put my third husband in the grave nearly a half century ago, and I hardly feel the need to go off myself, although in my case—unlike yours—hardly anyone would notice. Checking out early just isn't *done*, my boy. It's plain rude and disrespectful to the living, it's downright lazy, and it's like turning off a movie midway through. You have to see things through to the end."

Rita could tell Orlando was floored. He had probably never exchanged two words with the widow in his life, and here she was interrupting his suicide plot as if she were merely catching a schoolboy in the act of teepeeing the high school.

"Now," the widow said, her schoolmarm voice dropping lower, "give me the gun before you hurt yourself. I'm sure you haven't the foggiest idea how to handle a firearm, whereas I was the Morris County Ladies' Rifle Shooting champion of 1937."

And, like a schoolboy, he meekly obeyed.

Epilogue

In all the commotion of driving to South Carolina and back, springing Vinnie and Rocco from jail, solving a murder, and preventing a suicide, Rita had almost forgotten that Easter was just three days away.

Which meant that she was going to put the most multitasking Millennial to shame.

"Oh, Marion," she trilled into the phone as she leaned over the stove to start the filling for her *pastiera napoletana*, the most traditional Italian dessert for Easter. It took three whole days to make, tasted a little like rice pudding stuffed into a pie crust, and reputedly was the one thing that made Maria Teresa of Naples, "the queen who never smiled," actually break into a grin.

"I need you to activate the Ladies of Charity phone tree," Rita said. "I need someone to bring a casserole to Orlando Rinaldi every day."

"But is that really necessary, Rita? The man does own a restaurant, you know."

Rita stirred together dense, nutty wheatberries with whole milk and butter from the local creamery.

"It's not about the food, Marion." Rita held a gloriously golden Meyer lemon over the saucepan and attacked it with her zester, sending tiny golden flecks raining down into the mixture like gold fairy dust. "It's the thought that counts. He's grieving, you know. I don't want him all alone without someone checking on him."

Rita did not confide her darkest fears to Marion—that Orlando would try to take his life again. Unbeknownst to Marion, the Ladies of Charity would function more as a subtle suicide watch than anything else.

"Oh, I see," Marion clucked. "Well, I'm sure some of the widows would be very eager. Now, Sandra is about his age and very attractive...."

Rita laughed. It felt good to be carefree and chatting with Marion again, secure in the knowledge that the case was closed and Jack was locked up. "And be sure to call my sister," Rita said. "I can almost bet she'll volunteer for at least two shifts."

Rose was a member of the Ladies of Charity in name only, having joined for the rather mercenary reason that she thought it might get her a listing or two, but Rita was quite sure she'd make an exception this time.

Marion giggled. "Look at you, Rita. Lent's not even over yet, and you're already scheming."

"Oh, no—I'm staying out of the romance business from now on. Rose is on her own!"

She called Bianca next. "I think you should stay with your father for a few days, *cara*. Just—in case. He's very upset, you know. Men hide it well, but a loss like this hits them hard."

To her relief, Bianca readily agreed. Then she said something that really surprised Rita. "Vinnie asked me out, you know."

"My Vinnie?"

"Yeah."

Rita removed the mixture, which was now the consistency of oatmeal, from the stove and plopped down into a kitchen chair. So Vinnie was "One Confused Dude in Love with a Cougar."

"And what did you say?" Rita asked weakly. "I hope you let him down easily. He's very sensitive, really."

"I didn't."

"Didn't what, *cara?*"

"Turn him down. I figured that if my dad could find happiness with Greta—well, before Jack ruined everything—despite their age difference, a thirteen-year age gap isn't that big of a deal. And he is very sweet."

Rita was relieved that they were having this conversation over the phone rather than in person so that Bianca could not see that her eyeballs were about to roll right out of their sockets. She could not imagine what Bianca and Vinnie could possibly have in common. She also could not imagine that it would end well.

Rita was just about to ask Bianca where they were going to go on their ill-fated date, but then thought better of it. Because if Rita knew where it was, she would be tempted to just *happen* to pass by there at around the same time....

No, she was not going to intervene.

She mentally revised that: she was not going to *meddle.*

"Oh, look at the time!" Rita exclaimed "I'm so sorry, Bianca, but I've got to swing by St. Vincent's for confession."

Father De La Pasqua was scheduled to hear confessions from two to four that afternoon, and Rita, much to the chagrin of those in line behind her, took nearly the entire allotted two hours. When she finished, she peered through the wooden grille into the silence. Had her confession gone on so long that he had actually fallen asleep?

"*Allora, Padre?*" she prodded him. She always said her confession in Italian, as it somehow made her feel even more guilt-ridden and contrite. "What's my penance?"

She wasn't quite sure what she expected. Perhaps he would start with a sigh of exasperation, followed by a conclusion that she was beyond redemption and had failed spectacularly in her attempts not to meddle. Perhaps he would order her to undertake a pilgrimage to Rome. Actually, she was kind of hoping for the pilgrimage, as then she would have an unimpeachable reason to prod Sal to take her to Italy. And Rome was full of breezy piazzas, breathtaking art, and sinful gelaterias, and so close to the sun-drenched pebbly beaches of the Cinque Terre, the rugged Amalfi Coast, and the glorious, cypress-lined hills of Tuscany. Perhaps after the pilgrimage she could hole up in a Tuscan *agriturismo*, maybe one with a pool and a quaint little vineyard....

Father De La Pasqua cleared his throat. "*Niente.*"

"*Niente?*"

She could not believe she was hearing him right. Surely, she must perform some sort of penance. She had broken her Lenten pledge at nearly every opportunity.

"You forget, Rita, that Jesus broke all kinds of Jewish laws. He healed the sick on the Sabbath. He performed miracles on the Sabbath. He hobnobbed with prostitutes. But he was faithful to a higher principle: do unto others as you would have them do unto you. There's nothing wrong with helping your son with a sticky, er, legal situation—"

Rita smiled, grateful for Father De La Pasqua's delicacy.

"—or giving your husband's cousin some tips about how to treat his wife better and then driving him home. That's teaching someone how to fish, not handing him the fish."

Rita frowned. It seemed as though Father De La Pasqua was getting terribly confused with his metaphors. As Rita recalled it, while Jesus gave his Sermon on the Mount, his disciples were doing just that—handing everyone free fish that miraculously kept multiplying.

"Meddling," the priest was saying, "is manipulating the situation. Making the participants feel like they have no choice but to do what you want. Making the choice for them." He sighed. "I'm not giving you penance because there's nothing to forgive. All I hope is that you learned something from this. Did you?"

Rita rocked back on the hard wooden kneeler. Even with a cushion on top, it dug into her kneecaps and made her acutely aware of her sixty-seven years.

"Yes, I think so," Rita said slowly. "I've been coming to church every week for sixty-seven years, which means I've heard the reading about taking out the plank in your own eye before removing the sliver in your neighbor's eye at least twenty-two times. But I've never really known what that meant—I've never felt it viscerally, that is—until I had to confront my feelings for Viola. I hated her so much I wanted her to be guilty of murder. I thought she was guilty, was convinced of it, even when the evidence didn't quite fit, because, see, someone like her just *had* to be guilty of something that terrible."

"And why," he said softly, "did you hate her so much?"

"Because she had the sliver."

They were silent for a moment. She could hear his shallow breathing on the other side of the screen.

"And you had the plank?" he asked gently.

"Something like that," she said. "Viola was intervening in everyone's lives in the worst way—blackmailing them—because she wanted power. She needed to feel important. And getting into her twisted mind was like holding up some sort of fun house mirror to myself, only it was horrible to see. I thought I acted from the purest of motives—I wanted my daughter to be happy in love, I wanted my son to be successful—but the truth is I also want to know that I still matter to them, that I'm still at the center of their lives."

"So she manipulates people out of hate or jealousy, and you manipulate them out of love."

"Or fear," she said, "of losing that love."

"I think that's the last thing you need to fear." His voice was warm and gentle. "Have faith, Rita, and walk with hope in the Lord."

And with that, she was dismissed.

She walked out into the blinding sunshine. The birds were singing, and the daffodils were blooming.

"No time like the present," she said to herself as she took out her phone to call Gina.

Rita fasted dutifully on Good Friday, went to Mass at three o'clock, and spent the rest of the afternoon making the pastry dough for the *pastiera* crust and mixing its ricotta filling with sugar, vanilla, cinnamon, and orange blossom water. Her kitchen smelled heavenly, and her stomach growled with hunger.

On Saturday, Gina came over to help her with the final preparations for their Easter celebration. They assembled the *pastiera*, brushed the flakey crust with egg wash, and slid it in the oven. Then they turned their attention to marinating the lamb, making more pastry dough for the *torta pasqualina* (savory Easter pie), and making the dove-shaped *columba pasquale* that they would eat for Easter breakfast.

They were just adding in the *fiori di Sicilia*, that mysterious elixir that smelled of citrus and vanilla, to the *columba* dough when Rita finally got up the nerve to tell Gina that Jack had been arrested for murder, in no small part due to Rita's actions.

Gina froze and then reacted in the way Rita had least expected.

She laughed.

"Um, Ma, don't you think I already know that? I mean, how slow do you think the gossip travels in Acorn Hollow?"

Rita let the wooden spoon sink into the dough. "You're not mad?"

Gina shook her head. She formed a ball with her hands and then turned it out on the floured butcher block to knead. "Maybe I should let you pick them after all." She pushed down hard with the heel of her hand and then turned the dough ninety degrees. "I mean, the last one you picked out for me *only* turned out to be a drug dealer. And you did warn me about Jack."

"But I got it all wrong," Rita said. "I warned you that he was a simpleton—which turned out to be completely untrue. He was a brilliant, calculating killer—and he nearly got away with it."

Gina sighed and shrugged. "Well, you were right that he was too young for me."

She was really putting her shoulders into it now, rocking back and forth rhythmically.

"You know why Morgan dumped Matt Peruzzi?" Gina said. "She said he was boring. Stone, cold boring. Like being with a ninety-year-old. That's what she said."

"But that's ridiculous," Rita fumed. "Matt—"

She was about to list all the reasons he was not boring, the way a debate champ might launch into an argument, overwhelming the opposition with the sheer number of salient points that were hard to refute. But then she stopped herself. It did not matter whether Morgan found him boring. It only mattered whether Gina found him boring, and she would not try to make up her daughter's mind on that point.

"Yes?" Gina looked amused. "Matt what?"

"Matt is a nice boy. That's all. I wish him the very best."

"With me?"

"That's for you to decide, *cara*."

Gina laughed and held a hand to her mother's forehead. "Are you feeling all right, Ma?"

"Better than ever, *cara*."

Gina looked as though she might cry. "I love you, Ma."

"*Ti amo, figlia*."

Easter was divine. Rita awoke in the Easter spirit and belted out aria after aria as she stuffed the artichokes, assembled her spring citrus salad, and whipped up the egg, ricotta, and chard filling for her *torta pasqualina*. As it turned a lovely golden brown in the oven, she enjoyed a traditional Easter breakfast of fresh-baked *columba* (slathered, in her case, with clotted cream, honey, and homemade marmalade) washed down with a steaming hot cappuccino. She and Gina beamed at each other across the breakfast table, and all was right with the world.

She floated through church high on the idea of new beginnings and then raced home to dust her *pastiera* with powdered sugar and roast the lamb.

When she saw her *famiglia* around the table—Sal, Marco, Susan, Gina, Vinnie, Rose, Calvino, and Concetta—her heart was so full of love it almost burst.

"*Un brindisi*," she said, and they all raised their glasses. "To my wonderful, big, messy Italian family—and to new beginnings."

Gina smiled shyly at her mother over her glass, Vinnie turned red and looked down (did he know that she knew about Bianca?), and Marco and Susan looked quizzically at each other while Calvino and Concetta stared lovingly into each other's eyes.

There was a chorus of "*salute*" and "*cin cin.*" Then everyone clinked glasses, and the spell was broken.

"Speaking of new beginnings," Sal said, shooting a mischievous wink across the table at Rita, "or at least changes of pace, I thought you might need a little break, Rita."

Rita blinked. A break? What was her husband talking about? She hoped Calvino hadn't talked him into a timeshare in Florida with some kind of high-pressure sales pitch. She had no desire to lounge around the pool, sandwiched between leather-skinned senior citizens who bragged endlessly about their grandchildren while pitying her for having none.

Or did he mean that it was time to retire? Was he worried she was working too hard? Her heart sank. She could not give up her job. It was her lifeline to the larger world, and she thrived on the excitement. She swore that all the adrenaline had made her ten years younger.

"Only for two weeks," he said reassuringly. He reached into his breast pocket and pulled out something that looked like tickets and waved them across the table at her. "To *bella Italia!*"

"*Italia!*" she screamed. She stood up and practically lunged across the table in her excitement.

"Oh, great!" Calvino said. "You guys are gonna come along with me and Concetta. That'll be real swell..."

Rita's heart sank for just a moment. She had grown fond of Calvino in the past few weeks, but Easter dinner was one thing and a trip quite another....

"Calvino," Sal said. "This is no double date. This is our second honeymoon! We're going to Rome, Florence, Venice, this little vineyard in Tuscany...."

"*Toscana!*"

Rita could see it now, a sweet little stone cottage with a terracotta roof and a flagstone terrace leading to an aquamarine pool. They'd sit by the pool, dipping real Florentine *cantucci* into a sweet *vin santo* made right on the premises. They'd stroll through vineyards, help the owners press their olives and cure their *caciocavallo* cheese. They'd fall asleep to the sound of the breeze rustling through the cypress trees and awake to the sound of bird song and the aroma of fresh, strong coffee.

Rita swept Sal up in her arms, and they broke into a spontaneous *tarantella* all around the dining room table, while her family burst into an off-key rendition of "That's Amore."

It was the best ending to the best—and strangest—Easter season she had ever had.

Ripped from the Pages of Rita Calabrese's
"Top Secret" Recipe Book...

Lasagna

Lasagna is a very traditional Carnevale dish, as it was a good way to use up meat, fat, and dairy products before the season of Lent began! Every family has its own recipe, and there are numerous regional differences: in Naples, it can include sausage, small fried meatballs, and hard-boiled eggs, among other ingredients, while in Emilia-Romagna, often considered Italy's gastronomic capital, it is often made with green (i.e. spinach) lasagna noodles and bechamel sauce. There are a few constants, however: the liberal use of cheese, the size and shape of the lasagna noodles, and the fact that the dish is always baked (*al forno*).

The benefit of being Italian-American is that I'm not beholden to any particular region, so this is a fairly typical American version. However, I am quite partial to using the egg-enriched lasagna noodles (although there's no reason for them to be green) typical in northern Italy. They really enhance the flavor and texture of the dish!

1 ½ pounds ground beef
¾ cup chopped onions
3 cloves of garlic, minced
15 oz. peeled diced plum tomatoes
12 oz. tomato paste
12 oz. tomato sauce
3 tbsp. Italian parsley, divided
2 tbsp. sugar
2 1/2 tsp. salt, divided
1 tbsp. finely chopped basil
3 tsp. oregano, divided

15 oz. full-fat ricotta cheese
½ cup grated Parmesan cheese
2 cups mozzarella cheese, shredded and divided
12 long, thin egg lasagna noodles

Preheat oven to 350 degrees.

Place onions and ground beef in a saucepan and heat until the onions are translucent and the beef is browned. Add garlic and continue to sauté for one more minute. Drain fat.

Add tomatoes, breaking them up with a fork. Stir in tomato sauce, 2 tbsp. parsley, sugar, 1 tsp. salt, basil, and 2 tsp. oregano. Bring to a boil, then lower to a simmer.

While the sauce is simmering, bring a large pot of salted water to boil add the lasagna noodles, cooking until al dente. Remove from heat, drain water, and set aside.

In a separate bowl, mix ricotta, parmesan, 1 cup of mozzarella, and remaining salt and oregano.

Now, in a large glass baking dish, assemble the lasagna. Spread a layer of sauce, then lasagna, then cheese, and repeat until ending with a layer of sauce.

Top with remaining mozzarella and bake, uncovered, for 45-50 minutes.

Sanguinaccio Dolce

Don't let the name put you off!

Yes, *sanguinaccio* means "big blood" and refers to blood sausage, but *sanguinaccio dolce* (often now confusingly shortened to just "*sanguinaccio*") refers to a rich, spicy chocolate pudding traditionally made with pigs' blood. Because the pig butchering season coincided with the Carnevale holiday season, this dessert came to be associated with Carnevale.

These days, the traditional treat is hard to come by: for sanitary reasons, Italy banned the sale of pigs' blood in 1992. But the good news is that you can make this dessert without its most famous ingredient, and it's just as good (maybe better to modern palates). Sure, it lacks the salty-sweet metallic taste that the blood gives it, but the cinnamon and cloves still give it an unusual spicy twist.

If you don't like spicy chocolate, just omit the cinnamon and cloves.

¾ cup cocoa
¼ cup flour
1 cup powdered sugar
1 tsp. cinnamon
½ tsp. salt
¼ tsp. ground cloves
2 tsp. pure vanilla extract
2 cups whole milk
4 oz. bittersweet baking chocolate (70%), chopped
2 tbsp. butter

Candied lemon or orange peels (optional)

In a large saucepan, mix together the cocoa, flour, sugar, spices, salt, and vanilla, removing any lumps. Add the milk in ¼-cup increments, mixing well after each addition. Put on saucepan on low-medium heat, stirring constantly, until the mixture is thick and glossy, about 10 minutes. Then remove the saucepan from the stove and mix in butter and chopped bittersweet chocolate until smooth and thoroughly combined.

Pour the mixture into six individual ramekins (or, for a very traditional touch, hollowed-out orange peels) and chill in the refrigerator.

Garnish with candied lemon or orange peels if desired.

Curried Sweet Potato Soup

This soup is perfect for Meatless Mondays or simple Lenten soup suppers—but to make it truly vegetarian, you will need to substitute vegetarian stock for the chicken stock (although I think it tastes better with chicken stock).

¼ cup extra virgin olive oil
2 yellow onions, chopped
1 tsp. salt
1 tsp. freshly ground black pepper
5 cloves garlic, minced
2 tsp. curry powder
1 tsp. ground coriander
6 cups chicken stock
3 large sweet potatoes, peeled and diced
2 large carrots, peeled and chopped
1 tbsp. fresh lime juice
1 bunch cilantro
½ cup toasted pumpkin seeds

Heat the olive oil in a big soup pot. Add onions, salt, and pepper, stirring until onions are translucent. Stir in curry powder, coriander, and garlic, and stir for 1 minute. Add stock, sweet potatoes, carrots, and lime juice. Cover and bring to a boil until the sweet potatoes are tender when pierced with a fork (about 25 minutes).

Purée the soup with a stick blender. Garnish with chopped cilantro and pumpkin seeds.

Ramp Butter

Essentially wild onions, ramps are probably the foraged food most likely to grace a gourmand's table. Unlike domesticated onions, however, the bulb is tiny and most of what is eaten are the pungent green leaves. Ramp butter is a simple way to use and preserve fresh ramps, and it's delicious on fish.

2 sticks butter
2 tbsp. heavy cream
5 ramps
1 lime, juiced
3 cloves garlic, minced
Sea salt to taste

Remove slimy outer coating on the bulb of each ramp. Rinse ramps well and cut off the bottom root of each bulb. Chop entire ramp (white and green parts) coarsely and pulse in food processor until reduced to very small pieces. In a large bowl, cream the butter until soft. Then add in ramp pieces, heavy cream, lime juice, garlic and sea salt. Stir well to combine.

Use liberally and enjoy! This makes a lot so simply form the unused ramp butter into logs, wrap in wax paper, seal tightly, and freeze. Later, you can cut slices off the log and either use it to sauté vegetables or other ingredients in a frying pan or place directly on fish, chicken, or meat before baking in the oven (no need to thaw it first).

Columba (Italian Easter Bread)

This bread takes its name from its shape: a dove (*columba*), a traditional symbol of Easter, hope, and rebirth in Italy. It tastes rather like its Christmas counterpart, Panettone, and although it originated in Lombardy, it's now found throughout Italy during the Easter season. Note that if you want to serve this on Easter morning, you'll need to start the bread on Friday evening!

For the biga (overnight starter):

1 cup all-purpose flour
½ cup cool water
1/8 teaspoon instant yeast

For the dough:

2 ¼ cups all-purpose flour
1 ¼ tsp. salt
1 tbsp. instant yeast
1/3 cup sugar
4 tbsp. butter, at room temperature
2 eggs
1 egg yolk (save egg white for topping)
1 tsp. Fiori di Sicilia or orange blossom oil
1 tsp. pure vanilla extract
1 orange peel, grated
1 cup dried sour cherries, chopped

For the topping:

1 egg white

4 tbsp. slivered almonds
4 tbsp. pearl sugar

In a medium bowl, mix together the biga ingredients, cover with a clean dishcloth, and let rise at room temperature for at least 15 hours.

Combine the biga, which should be foaming and bubbly, with all of the dough ingredients except the orange rind and the dried cherries. Knead until shiny and elastic. (If using a dough hook, use medium speed for about 12 minutes.)

Knead in the orange peel and cherries. Form dough into a large ball and place in a large clean bowl to rise until at least doubled in size, roughly 3 hours at a temperature of 110 degrees F or so (either keep in slightly warmed oven, or place bowl on top of a large pot of water that has been boiled and removed from the stove).

Line a baking sheet with parchment paper. Use just over half the dough to form the "body" of the dove and place on the parchment paper. Then created two "wings" from the remaining dough and gently join them to the main body. (If you are more of a Martha Stewart type, you can purchase a *columba* mold online or in specialty shops and use that instead.)

Cover baking sheet with a clean dishcloth and allow to rise for 2 hours at 110 degrees F.

Preheat oven to 375 F. Brush raw loaf with egg white, then sprinkle almonds and pearl sugar on top. Bake for

15 minutes, then reduce heat to 350 F and bake for an additional 20 minutes, tented for the last 10 minutes.

Enjoy toasted, use in French toast, or serve with sweetened whipped mascarpone cheese, butter, or clotted cream, and with marmalade or cherry jam for a delicious Easter morning treat!

Torta Pasqualina (Italian Savory Easter Pie)

Think of this as a more festive version of a quiche, but with a top crust and with eggs—an ancient symbol of spring and rebirth—figuring even more prominently than usual.

For the crust:

2 ½ cups all-purpose flour
1 tsp. salt
2 tbsp. granulated sugar
1 cup unsalted butter, cut into very small cubes and chilled until very, very cold (but not frozen)
½ cup ice water (may not use all of it)

For the filling:

2 tbsp. olive oil
2 bunches Swiss or rainbow chard, stems and ribs removed
1 sweet yellow onion
15 oz. whole milk ricotta
½ cup grated Parmesan cheese
12 eggs, divided
¼ tsp. ground nutmeg
Salt and pepper to taste

In a medium bowl, mix flour, salt, and sugar until combined. Then cut in butter with a pastry blender until the butter is reduced to tiny, scattered pea-sized pieces.

Then drizzle in ice water slowly, incorporating with a fork until the dough starts to stick together. Using your hands, form the dough into two balls. Wrap each individually in plastic wrap and place in the refrigerator.

While the dough is chilling, dice the onion and wash and chop the chard, squeezing out all the water you can. Then heat oil in a large frying pan and sauté the onions until soft and translucent. Remove onions, add more oil, toss in chard, season it with salt and pepper, and sauté the chard until wilted; work in batches if necessary.

Remove the chard from the heat. In a large mixing bowl, combine the ricotta, Parmesan, nutmeg, and 4 beaten eggs. Then add in the chard and onions and mix well to distribute the chard and onions evenly throughout the cheese mixture.

Preheat the oven to 375 degrees F. Remove dough from the refrigerator and roll out each crust. Place bottom crust in 9-inch pie pan. Scoop filling on top, then use a wooden spoon to make eight divots in the filling. Crack an egg into each divot. (These will turn out like hard-boiled eggs when cooked, and you want them evenly spaced so that if you cut the pie into eight slices, everyone will get an egg.) Then put the top pie crust on top.

Place the pie pan on a baking sheet and bake for 45 minutes until golden brown.

This dish can be the first course of an Easter dinner. Alternatively, serve with a garden salad for a delightful light lunch!

ITALIAN-ENGLISH GLOSSARY

(Note: Only terms that are not immediately obvious from the text are included here. Approximate pronunciation shown in parentheses.)

Accidenti! (Ach-ee-DENT-ee!) – Literally, accident. Equivalent although perhaps stronger than the English "oh, no!"

Acque alte (AK-qway AL-tay) – High water. The term the Venetians use when their city floods after heavy rains – an increasingly common occurrence.

Bistecca alla fiorentina (bis-TAY-ka a-la fee-or-en-TEEN-a) – Literally "a Florentine steak." A T-bone steak that is char-grilled on the outside and very rare on the inside; a specialty of Tuscany and, in particular, Florence (hence the name).

Brindisi (brin-dee-zee) – Toast (i.e., propose a toast).

Briscola (BREES-co-la) – Italian card game.

Buon giorno (BWON JOR-no) – Good day (a greeting).

Buona sera (BWONA SARE-ah) – Good evening.

Cantucci (Can-TOO-chee) – Almond biscotti originally from Tuscany, traditionally served for dessert with a sweet vin santo (see below).

Caro/cara (CAR-o, CAR-a) – Dear (for a man if ending in -o, for a woman if ending in -a). A term of endearment.

Certo/certo che non! (CHER-toe, CHER-toe kay non) – Certainly/of course, certainly not!

Che voce bello! (Kay VO-che BEL-lo) – What a beautiful voice!

Che c'e? (Kay chay?) – What is it? What's wrong?

Ci vediamo pronto (Chee vay-dee-A-mo PRON-to) – We'll see each other soon.

Cretino (Cray-TEEN-o) – Idiot.

Dai! (DIE!) – Come on!

È morta (Ay MOR-ta) – She's dead.

Mangia! (MAHN-jee-ah) – Eat! (command)

Mille grazie per tutto (MIL-lay GRATZ-ee-ay pear TOO-toe) – Many (literally, a thousand) thanks for everything.

Mi dispiace (Mee dis-pee-A-chay) – Sorry (literally, it displeases me).

Niente (nee-EN-tay)—Nothing.

Non ti preocupare (Non pre-oc-u-PAR-ay) – Don't worry.

Nonna (NO-na) – Grandma.

Per fortuna (Pear for-TOON-a) – Fortunately.

Per piacere (Pear Pee–a-CHAIR-ay) – Please (more pleading than "per favore").

Pettegolando (Pet-ay-go-LAN-do) – Gossiping.

Pignoli (Pin-NYO-lee) – Pine nut cookies.

Poverino/poverina (Po-ver-EE-no/Po-ver-EE-na) – Poor (not low-income, but to be pitied).

Principesa (Prin-chee-PAY-za) – Princess.

Sii corragioso (SEE cor-a-JO-zo) – Be brave (courageous). "Buck up."

Spaghetti alle vongole (Spa-GET-tee a-lay VON-go-lay) – Spaghetti noodles with clams.

Stonzo (STRONTZ-o) – A not very nice word for a not very nice person.

Struffoli (STROOF-o-lee) – Italian Christmastime treat made with fried dough and honey.

Tarantella (tar-an-TELL-a)—A kind of folk dance popular in Southern Italy, characterized by a fast tempo and usually accompanied by tambourines.

Ti amo (Tee A-mo) – I love you.

Vin santo (Vin SAN-to) – A sweet wine from Tuscany, traditionally served after dinner with *cantucci*. Literally, "holy wine."

ABOUT THE AUTHOR

Maureen Klovers is the author of the Jeanne Pelletier mystery series set in Washington, D.C., as well as the memoir *In the Shadow of the Volcano: One Ex-Intelligence Official's Journey through Slums, Prisons, and Leper Colonies to the Heart of Latin America*. A confirmed Italophile, Maureen has studied Italian in Rome and enjoys testing Italian recipes (many of which make their way into Rita's cookbook!). She lives outside of Washington, D.C., with her husband, Kevin; her daughter, Kathleen; and their black Labrador Retriever, Nigel.

For more information on Maureen and her writing, or to schedule her for a book signing or book club event, please visit her Facebook author page or email her at maureenkloverswrites@gmail.com.

AND IF YOU ENJOYED THIS BOOK...

Please post a review on amazon.com, goodreads.com, or your own blog! Thank you!